FOUR RODE HOME

Holly and Roy decided to spend a holiday with a difference – a riding tour across southern England from the New Forest back home to Kent, and invite two friends, Rebecca and Clive, to join them. Their horses range from Rebecca's tall chestnut Baynard, to Holly's newly-acquired New Forest pony, Crumpet, only 13½ hands but intelligent and reliable. They plan to stay at youth hostels, and to keep to bridle-paths, quiet lanes and open ground while on the move, but it doesn't always work out that way.

Primrose Cumming knows this countryside, and gives accurate information on how to plan a holiday of this kind, as well as on horses and their management.

PRIMROSE CUMMING

Four rode home

 KNIGHT BOOKS

the paperback division of Brockhampton Press

*Because of the closure of some youth hostels and
the opening of new ones, some of the hostels referred
to in this book may no longer be in existence. For more
up-to-date information, the current Youth Hostels
Association Handbook should be consulted.*

SBN 340 03310 X

*This edition first published 1969 by Knight Books,
the paperback division of Brockhampton Press Ltd, Leicester*

*Printed in Great Britain by
Cox & Wyman Ltd, London, Reading and Fakenham*

First published by J. M. Dent & Sons Ltd, 1951

CONTENTS

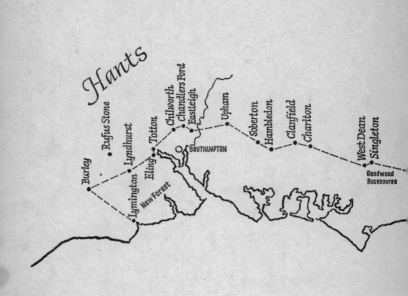

Hants

Burley • Rufus Stone • Lyndhurst • Lymington • Eling • Totton • Chilworth • Chandlers Ford • Eastleigh • Upham • Soberton • Hambledon • Clanfield • Charlton • West Dean • Singleton • Goodwood Racecourse

New Forest

○ SOUTHAMPTON

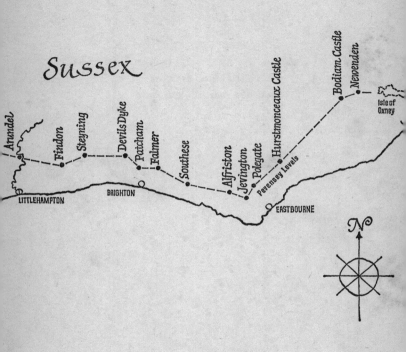

TO DAPHNE HAYNES
who also rode this way home

I

Plans for a journey

THE thudding of hoofs and the sharp smell of trodden grass rose on the soft spring air as two riders came cantering home. The green levels of Romney Marsh were kind to horses' legs and wind, and the skewbald and grey vied with each other for the lead. Home was Haffeneys, a farm standing on the very edge of the Marsh under the shelter of the uplands which rose behind it as steeply as a cliff. Holly and Roy Granger drew rein as they approached the tree-bordered canal and the track which would bring them to a cart bridge. They lost no time in resuming their talk, interrupted by the last canter.

'You see, if only we could have kept straight on instead of turning back we should be twenty miles away by now,' said Holly, dropping the rein on Kelly's collar-marked neck as the old grey cob lapsed into his usual plodding walk.

'H'm, well, fifteen,' said Roy, less given to flights of imagination.

'Anyhow, we should have got easily to the other side of the Marsh. And if we kept going day after day, why, we'd get right across England in time.'

'Yes, in time.' Roy agreed to this. 'But I suppose we'd have to come back one day.'

'Not till we'd ridden through lots of new country where we'd never been before – places with big rivers, and hills and forests and things.'

'Yes, and we could find our way by maps along tracks and bridle-paths and ways that have almost been forgotten.' Roy caught some of his sister's romance. 'It would be next best to pioneering.'

'And we'd sleep in a different place every night.'

'And never know from one day to the next exactly where we'd land up.'

'Oh, Roy, we simply must do it. Let's ask daddy again.'

'You know what he said last year when we wanted to go on a riding tour.'

'I know. But we're both a year older now, and most responsible, if only people would realize it.'

They had by now crossed the little-used canal and were turning in at the farm gate. The house, tile-hung and steep-roofed, looked out through the screen of wych-elms straight across the Marsh, while the farm buildings, tiled like the house, together with stacks of hay and straw, formed a little courtyard beside it. The yard was still muddy and cattle-stodged even at this time of the year. Kelly and Sarah, Roy's skewbald, broke into a little jog as they passed through the gate.

'I don't think Kelly would care much for your idea of going on and on – he always knows when it's time to turn for home,' remarked Roy. 'I say, Josh, do you know where dad is?'

His question was addressed to the little old cowman, busy slicing mangolds in an open-fronted lodge. Joshua was bent with rheumatism and a little deaf, but he made up for these handicaps by a lively and emphatic manner of speaking. He poured a string of epithets upon Sarah, who was gnawing a mangold, before replying:

'Gone down to the ferry to see Bert. Take that pestiferous circus animal away from my mangolds.'

'Let's go down there and ask him straight away,' suggested Holly.

But old Kelly jibbed at the idea of leaving the yard again. He knew his duties exactly: an early morning journey to the station with the milk churns, and one ride a day for Holly in the holidays and at week-ends. To go out for a second ride, as he thought, was a bad mistake in the routine, and he anchored himself firmly in the mud with his ears laid back. Urgings and pressure from his rider's heels only increased the ferocity of his expression.

'Please, Josh, come and lead him out!' shouted Holly.

Grumblingly Joshua hobbled round and laid hold of the bridle. Kelly gave him a murderous look, knowing he had met his match, lurched out of the ooze, and was sent on his way with an undignified slap.

''Bout time you two had some riding lessons!' Joshua shouted after them.

It was not far to the ferry, an old name for what was now another bridge across the canal. Just across here stood the straw-thatched hurdles which Bert, the looker, had put up to shelter the lambing ewes. The flock was spread out feeding, the young lambs looking as white as thorn blossom scattered over the vivid green grass. Gruff and Tim, Bert's two collies, gave short barks of greeting, not bothering to rise from where they lay beside their master's lunch haversack. Years of battling with the winds out on the Marsh had tanned Bert as brown as a sun-bather in August. At this time of the year he was out at night, too, and although he was not an old man, the deep wrinkles ran out fan-wise from the corners of his screwed-up eyes.

Mr Granger smiled and waved to his children as they trotted towards him over the turf, the grey cob and the patches of white on the skewbald showing up sharply against the misty green of the wych-elms, the children's faces rosy with riding in the light wind, and Holly's dark brown hair flying loose.

'Had a good ride?' he asked as they drew up.

'Not bad,' said Roy. 'But we can't find any new ways.'

'Daddy, how old did you say you were when you set sail for the Argentine?'

'Seventeen and two days. Now, what's this in aid of?'

Mr Granger cocked an eyebrow inquiringly at his daughter as he patted Kelly's neck.

'Well then, don't you think we're old enough now to go on a riding tour next hols?'

'A riding tour!' exclaimed Bert. 'Haven't you got all the Marsh and half the Weald to go gallivanting over?'

'Where were you thinking of going, the Rockies or the Texas ranges?' asked Mr Granger, and Bert laughed.

'Oh, we only meant in England,' said Roy, pretending to take his father seriously, 'as we're neither of us seventeen yet.'

'We do want to ride somewhere where we've never been before,' begged Holly.

Seeing their earnestness Mr Granger dropped his joking tones.

'I'm not saying that you couldn't look after yourselves all right on a riding tour, but have you thought how much it would cost?'

'N-no. Not exactly.'

'Well, there aren't many hotels nowadays where you can put up for less than a pound a night.'

'They say it's twenty-five shillings down at the George,' volunteered Bert. 'That's just bed and breakfast, not allowing for your supper.'

'There you are! Then you'd want food in the middle of the day and a place for the horses at night. Why, it would run into over thirty shillings a day each. At least twenty-one pounds a week for the pair of you, and you wouldn't get very far in that time, not there and back. Sorry, old things, but that's too much to pay just for a holiday.'

Very much cast down, Holly and Roy rode back to Haffeneys. Kelly and Sarah did not share their depression, but on the contrary radiated satisfaction at their speedy return.

'I don't see how we'll ever be able to go,' said Holly dolefully.

'I think it's stupid, costing so much,' said Roy, who had been making private calculations. 'After all, if we went out riding each day for a week, taking sandwiches, and only coming home for supper, bed and breakfast, it wouldn't cost anything like thirty shillings a day each, so why on earth should going on from place to place make so much difference?'

'I suppose it means clean sheets every night instead of once a week, but they can't cost all that to wash.'

Gloomily they unsaddled Kelly and Sarah, and led them out to the hummocky field behind the barn. Sarah rolled with grunts of pleasure, destroying in a minute half an hour's hard grooming. Kelly, more careful of his elderly frame, had a long drink from the stone trough, and then contented himself with a good shake, sending out a cloud of dust and white hairs upon the wind.

'We're lucky, really, to be able to ride at all,' said Roy, trying to look on the bright side. 'If we didn't have Kelly in the first place for the milk, and dad hadn't done that lucky swop with the dealer of two bull calves and an old cow for Sarah, we should only have had the bikes.'

'Bikes! I've got an idea. How much money have you got?'

'About fifteen bob. A little more with what a chap at school owes me on the ferret we bought between us.'

'Can't you sell your share of the ferret to him?'

'Not very well. He's got nowhere to keep it, and anyhow it's a polecat, and I'd rather not give up my half.'

'I've got about twenty-five shillings, mostly in postal orders from my birthday. That's nearly the price of one night's stay. I vote we sell our bikes to make up the rest.'

'How are we going to get to the station every day for school?'

'We could start a bit earlier and walk. It'll soon be the end of the term anyhow.'

'But who'd buy 'em?'

'Oh, don't be such a wet blanket! We'll ask Cecil. He belongs to a touring club, and goes out cycling nearly every week-end, so he's bound to know where we can sell them.'

Holly was thrilled with her scheme. She ran down to the farm to look for Cecil, their young tractor-driver, leaving Roy to follow more slowly with the bridles, the reins of which always got entangled round his legs. But it was now after midday, and being a Saturday all the farm men had gone home.

So they went along to Cecil's home, a cottage a short way along the canal bank. He was used to being consulted on matters of importance, for he had a number of qualifications, such as being able to drive a tractor wherever it was mechanically possible for one to go, an unerring hand and eye at darts, and a determination to keep up with the times. He was a Londoner by birth, his family having been evacuated during the war, and this fact gave a spice of sharp good humour to his advice. They found him in the woodshed tightening the chain of his blue and silver racing bicycle. Holly came straight to the point.

'We want to sell our bikes, Cecil. How much are they worth, and who would buy them?'

Cecil whistled.

'Sudden, ain't it?'

'We've got to make money quickly to go on a riding tour these hols.'

'But if you sell yer bikes you can't go on tour.'

'It's not a bicycle tour. We want to go on Kelly and Sarah,' Roy explained.

'I can't see old Kelly getting far; he'll be back home sharp by feed time on the first day.'

'Kelly's our business.' Holly was slightly nettled. 'We want you to tell us about selling the bikes.'

'But none of my pals ride that sort of bike. They want one like mine to do seventy or eighty miles a day.'

'But there must be some people who want ordinary respectable bikes to go shopping and visiting their aunts on,' persisted Holly.

'Maybe, but I don't mix with them sort. Wot d' you want so much dough for when you can manage OK on a few bob a day?'

'But that's the trouble, Cecil. Hotels are terribly expensive.'

'You don't want no blooming hotels, not when you're all dirty orf the road and stinking of horses into the bargain. Wot you want are youth hostels – four shillings a night, and a bit more for grub.'

'Cecil, that can't be true!'

'You bet it is, or I wouldn't go.'

'Do they give you enough to eat?' asked Roy.

'You can take your own grub and cook it yourself, free of charge. Or you can have canteen meals, and they expect you to come in hungry.'

'Of *course*! Hostels are the proper places for hikers and

mountaineers and people like us,' said Holly. 'Why didn't we think of that before? Do tell us some more.'

'Ain't got time now. I'm orf for a week-end spin d'rec'ly after dinner. But you can read this. It's got all you want to know.'

Cecil fished an oil-stained booklet from his saddlebag. Holly and Roy meandered home reading it. Amid squeaks of excitement from Holly they discovered that the charges were even less to people under sixteen, and also that most of the hostels were right out in the best countryside. Then Roy discovered a rough map showing the distances from one hostel to the next, and they immediately began to follow out a route. They had got to the borders of Wales in this manner when Roy said:

'But we still don't know if we'll be allowed to go.'

'Daddy practically said we could – it was only the cost he minded,' said Holly. 'But this way we ought to be able to do it on twelve or thirteen bob a day.'

Just then Roy, who had chanced to glance up, gave a whistle.

'My hat! It's Aunt Edith and Uncle Bernard! I quite forgot to tell you they were coming over to lunch. Look, there's the car just turned in at the gate. I don't think they spotted us.'

'If we nip up the back way we can be washed and down again before lunch begins.'

They raced through the farmyard and round to the back of the house. There were no back stairs, but an emergency entrance could be made by climbing on to the water tank and then up the sloping larder roof to Roy's bedroom window. Seven minutes later a tolerably clean though rather damp and breathless pair meekly entered the dining-room where their elders were just sitting down to lunch.

'Why, I was almost certain I saw you along the lane a few minutes ago!' exclaimed Aunt Edith. 'I shall have to have my glasses altered, I'm afraid.'

Uncle Bernard waved vigorously to them as if they were separated by at least two fields instead of the width of the table.

But their attention was speedily drawn to a third visitor, a short, sturdily built young woman with a beaming face.

'You see, we've got Rebecca home,' said Aunt Edith.

Rebecca, their cousin, was a good deal older than either Holly or Roy. Years ago they would not have welcomed her much because she had been inclined to boss them about. An unimaginative, though cheerful, person, she had scoffed at their games of pirates and explorers, and because she wanted to be a gym mistress had insisted on drilling them mercilessly and making them perform painful gymnastic feats. However, she had changed her mind since those days and taken up nursing instead. Holly and Roy had only seen her at intervals during her training, and as they grew older had found her a less alarming and even an amusing companion.

'How long have you got?' asked Holly, as they took their places on each side of Rebecca.

'I've got the rest of my life, if I like. You see, I've finished my training.'

'She's passed all her exams and is a fully qualified nurse,' Aunt Edith put in proudly.

'More by luck than judgment, I can tell you. And now I'm going to have a couple of months at home to recover my equilibrium and forget all I've learnt before taking a job abroad.'

'Oh, you lucky beast!' sighed Holly.

'Lucky? I jolly well think I deserve it after spending the best years of my life slaving away in the grubbiest part of London, and never able to call my soul my own! And what do you think, a friend of daddy's has lent me a horse while I'm home. He's called Baynard, and he's quite the tallest horse in England. I split my jods the first time I tried to mount, so now I have to ride in slacks until they're mended.'

'Come with us on our riding tour,' said Roy.

'Oh, but I'd simply love to!' exclaimed Rebecca, all surprise. 'When are you going, and where?'

'We don't know that we are. Roy, you are an ass!' hissed Holly.

Roy blinked and covered his confusion with a vacant stare.

Fortunately their parents were all talking too hard to listen to the younger ones' conversation just then.

'We'll tell you after lunch,' whispered Holly. 'I warn you, there are the most frightful difficulties in the way.'

Directly after lunch they took Rebecca outside on the excuse of visiting the horses.

'Now please explain the mystery,' demanded Rebecca. 'Why am I one minute made all excited by being asked to go on a riding tour, and the next told that it's quite impossible?'

'Dad says it would cost too much.'

'That sounds pretty definite.'

'Ah, but since then we've had a brain-wave,' broke in Holly.

'Cecil did, you mean. He told us about youth hostels, which don't cost a quarter so much as pubs.'

'And what does uncle say to that?'

'That's the point. We haven't had a chance to ask him.'

'And that's why I made Roy shut up at lunch. It doesn't always do to spring things on daddy in front of a lot of people.'

'Well, I think there would be more chance of our being allowed to go if Rebecca came too,' said Roy. 'She's almost equal to a grown-up.'

'Thanks for those few kind words.'

'Would you mind youth hostels?' asked Holly.

'Why should I? I may feel a hundred just after a spell of night duty, but it doesn't last.'

'I didn't mean the youth part. It's just that I don't suppose they'd be frightfully luxurious.'

'Whatever do you take me for!' exploded Rebecca. 'Of course I'm all in favour of hostels. The only drawback I've ever heard is that it's difficult to wash because the water's usually cold and there are never enough basins.'

'Well, after all, it is meant to be a holiday,' said Roy.

The sound of voices had brought Sarah and Kelly trotting down to the gate to get the sugar lumps smuggled by Holly out of the dining-room cupboard.

'Sarah has improved since I saw her last,' remarked Rebecca. 'You'd only had her a little while, and she was rather thin with an awful scrubby half-grown mane standing up on end.'

'The trouble we had to make that mane turn over,' said Holly. 'In the end it took a bottle of setting lotion and two dozen dinkie curlers, and it was awfully expensive because the curlers weren't a bit of use afterwards, her hair was so stiff it bent them all.'

'And she looked a complete sissy with her hair in curlers,' said Roy. 'Old Josh called her a hussy.'

'I should have chopped it right off,' said Rebecca. 'My old man's got a hogged mane, though I must say a long one would help with the mounting.'

Standing just over fourteen and a half hands, Sarah was a strong little mare of unknown parentage. Her rather straight shoulders, thick neck, and large hoofs were offset by her beautiful skewbald markings, which included a map of Australia across her quarters and the British Isles on her near shoulder. There was a silver streak in her tail, and a broad white blaze ending in a triangular pink patch between her nostrils gave her a pert expression. She was both intelligent and good-tempered, and Roy, in his undemonstrative way, adored her.

Kelly might once have been a handsome cob, and he still had a certain air of dignity, despite a tendency to corpulence, with his bony hips and the yellowish wisp of hair drooping from his short dock. His eyes looked unusually dark, deep set under his broad white brow, and his lower lip was slightly pendulous and quivered if he was in any way put out. He usually won the trotting race at a gymkhana, his steady pace carrying him ahead of more dashing rivals who balked themselves by breaking step, but he refused to co-operate in any event to do with dropping things in buckets or dodging between posts. Such tricks had not formed part of his early training, and his logical mind saw no sense in performing them now.

When Sarah and Kelly had been sufficiently admired Rebecca returned to the subject of the riding tour, the thought of which appealed to her strongly after years of hospital routine.

'Where are you thinking of going?' she asked.

'Do you think we could get as far as Dartmoor?'

'If we had half a year to do it in!'

'Of course we couldn't really get as far as that, not with old Kelly,' said Roy.

'How many miles a day do you think we could do?'

'About twenty-five, I should say,' said Rebecca. 'Remember, it means going on day after day.'

'That wouldn't get us very far in a week.'

'Have you got any maps? We might get as far as the South Downs.'

'Yes, dad's got lots of ordnance maps, inch-to-the-mile ones, with footpaths and windmills and ancient monuments,' said Roy eagerly.

'Then let's go in and have a squint at them.'

There was no one in when they got back to the house, for Mr Granger had taken his brother on a tour of the farm, and their mother and Aunt Edith were looking at the bulbs in the garden. Roy got the maps out of the old press in the hall, and opened them out all over the sitting-room floor. It was his favourite hobby.

'The South Downs lie only just the other side of Pevensey Levels,' said Rebecca. 'But even that would take us at least two days, because it's mostly roads and hard lanes.'

'Here's a lovely long bridle-path,' said Holly, running her nail along a narrow white line.

'It's going in the wrong direction, you juggins!' said Roy. 'But there are bound to be some decent paths once we get to the downs.'

'Hallo, going on a journey?'

They had all been so absorbed in the maps that the return of their parents took them by surprise.

'South Downs, eh?' said Mr Granger. 'I thought you were going abroad, Rebecca?'

'Oh, daddy!' cried Holly, deciding in a flash that this was 'the moment', 'Rebecca's simply dying to go on a riding tour, 'cos it's her only chance just while she's at home and got a horse, and if we stay at youth hostels it'll cost only four shillings a night.'

'Well, I'll be –' gasped Rebecca, amazed at the way in which she had been made responsible for the idea, but Holly hurried on:

'It wouldn't come to a quarter as much as if we stayed at hotels. Oh, do say that we can go these hols! Uncle Bernard, make him say that we can go!'

'Now then, brother, how are you going to answer this broadside?' roared Uncle Bernard.

'Well, I'd like to know a bit more about this hostel idea before I open up,' replied Mr Granger.

Three voices promptly started to enlighten him. He held his head in bewilderment while his brother laughed. Picking their way gingerly over the Sussex Weald and the downs, the two mothers sought refuge in arm-chairs, while their husbands got down on their knees among the children. Mr Granger took out his glasses to study the maps more closely. This was his undoing. As both his children knew, he could not resist a map, and they speedily lured him off down lanes and bridle-paths.

'Do you really mean you want to go on riding day after day?' asked Aunt Edith in astonishment.

'However will you carry suit-cases?' asked their mother. 'And supposing you fall off or lose the horses?'

'We wouldn't take suit-cases, mummy. We'd have rucksacks or saddle-bags or something.'

'You're bound to get lost,' said Aunt Edith sadly.

'They couldn't get lost for long in England,' said Mr Granger. 'In fact, they shouldn't get lost at all with good maps like these to follow.'

'That means we can go!'

'Here, I never actually said that!'

'But you certainly gave that impression,' boomed Uncle Bernard. 'Let them go. They'll be much safer on horseback than flying around on bicycles. Horses can at least look where they're going.'

'And now that Rebecca's a real nurse she'll know what to do if they fall off,' said Mrs Granger, taking comfort.

'Suppose I fall off first! I've got the farthest to come down too.'

'What about the horses?' asked Roy. 'Do they have stabling at youth hostels?'

'I'm sure they don't,' said Rebecca. 'Because most people go there on foot or bicycle. We should have to rely on farmers to put them up.'

'I don't think Kelly and Sarah would like being in stables,' said Holly. 'They only come in at night during mid-winter. They'd much rather be turned out, and a field might be easier to get than a stable.'

'Would they get enough to eat?'

'If you go as near the end of the holidays as possible the grazing will be at its best,' said Uncle Bernard. 'They should be all right on grass.'

'Wait a minute, I've got a much better plan,' their father suddenly announced, and they looked at him a little apprehensively. 'I've been calculating these distances; it'll take you about two and a half days to reach good riding country, and the same to come back; that's the best part of a week gone without allowing for any delays like casting a shoe or missing your road. How would you like to start out from a good way away, say two hundred miles, and ride home?'

They stared at him in astonishment.

'But wouldn't that mean taking the horses by train? It would cost millions.'

'Don't jump to conclusions. Do you remember our old friends the Fowles who moved down near Lymington in the New Forest?'

'Yes, he used to wear a funny hat,' said Holly.

'A deer-stalker. Yes, well, I've bought a young bull that he's bred down there, and somehow that bull's got to be brought up here.'

'You don't mean we're to drive it back?'

'What would they say at the youth hostels if we arrived with a bull as well as three horses?'

'You silly children, of course the bull will come in a truck.

Fowle was going to arrange the transport, but it wouldn't cost any more to send the truck from this end, in which case it could take you and your horses down there.'

This opened up an entirely new prospect.

'Would three horses go in one truck?' asked Rebecca.

'Easily. Four in one the size of Tim Poulter's.'

'The New Forest!' breathed Holly. 'Why, that's one of the places I've always longed and longed to ride through.'

'There'll be wild ponies and deer,' said Roy.

'And perfectly frightful bogs,' said Rebecca.

The two mothers gave cries of dismay at that.

'Nothing's settled at all,' said Mr Granger hastily. 'For one thing, the Fowles may not want a horde of horses and riders descending on them, because it would mean staying the night there. So you'd better forget the whole thing entirely until I know for certain.'

2

On tenterhooks

IN spite of their father's injunction, Holly and Roy thought of
very little else but the riding tour for the rest of the term, while
Rebecca rang up nearly every other evening to ask if it had been
settled. Mr Granger remained maddeningly non-commital, and
made the same reply to all their inquiries:

'I told you to forget it for the time being. Concentrate on
your exams and get them over first.'

The bunch of children who travelled to and fro to school by
train usually congregated in one carriage, their racket dis-
couraging most other passengers from entering. On the last day
of term they were all more vocal than ever, boasting of what
they were going to do in the holidays. Up to now Holly had
kept quiet about their riding tour in case it failed to come off,
but Roy was not so afraid of being laughed at, and began to tell
the rest about their plans. Most of them agreed that it was a
wizard idea, but Ernest, the lanky son of a garage owner,
said:

'Catch me riding anything as antiquated as a horse! If I went
touring it 'ud be on a motor-bike.'

'You're not old enough to have a licence,' Roy squashed him.

'I wish I could go,' said a young boy called Clive, who was
sitting more quietly than the rest in a corner seat. 'A really long
journey would be just the thing for my pony.'

'Is that the grey pony that ran away and bucked you off at
the children's meet last Christmas?' asked Holly.

'Well, you see, I'd had measles,' he explained, flushing, 'and
Alaska had hardly been ridden for a month. Things like hunting go to her head, and turning for home excites her too. But

she'd be simply splendid on a riding tour, 'cos she never gets tired.'

'Well, come along with us, if we go,' said Roy.

'Ooh, may I really? I'd love to! I'm sure mummy and daddy would let me. They never know what to do with me in the holidays because they're always so busy with the poultry farm.'

When they got out at their station and were collecting their bicycles Holly said to Roy:

'Why on earth did you say that? Clive really thinks he can come.'

'I don't see why he shouldn't. He's quite a decent little chap.'

'But we don't even know that *we* are going yet!'

'Oh, he understood that it wasn't settled.'

'And then there's Rebecca; she won't want a kid like that tagging along.'

'What the dickens difference will it make to her? You're just creating a fuss about nothing. For heaven's sake pipe down, Hol!'

But once Holly had started to let off steam there was no stopping her. She had a habit of storing up her feelings until they got too much for her and then let them loose with a force that startled her hearers. She was furious about the casual way in which Roy had invited Clive as if it were no more than a picnic they were going on. He had done the same with Rebecca, but that by pure luck had turned to their advantage. The whole affair on which her heart was set was still so uncertain that this time his thoughtlessness seemed just asking fate to push it off its balance.

'You never will think before you start blabbing,' she continued to storm as they cycled along the bumpy lane. 'It was just the same when you told the gipsies they could camp on our land, and we had to get the police to move them. What will daddy say? And that pony of Clive's will probably kick in the truck and break one of our horses' legs. I expect you've wrecked the whole scheme for ever.'

Holly continued on this line right the way home while Roy whistled and peered into the dikes. At the gate they met the postman, who handed Holly a little packet of letters for Mr Granger. The one on top had a New Forest postmark. In a second her row with Roy was temporarily forgotten.

'It's from Mr Fowle! Quick, let's find daddy!'

Fortunately their father was just coming in for tea. He opened the envelope slowly, and read the slanting handwriting apparently unaware of the two pairs of eyes trained upon his face. Towards the end of the second page he began to smile.

'Well I'm jiggered! Old Charlie Fowle's home-bred heifer got a championship at the dairy show. He couldn't tell one end of a cow from the other when I first knew him.'

'But the riding tour – can we go?'

'Oh, that!' He reverted to the beginning of the letter. 'It's rather yes and no.' Even Roy began to fidget at that. 'He says it will be quite all right for you to come, and Mrs Fowle would be delighted to put you up for the night if you don't mind sleeping in the attics.'

'Hooray!' cried Holly, seizing Roy by the wrists and waltzing him round.

'But you said something about a "no",' Roy reminded him jerkily.

'Yes, and it's bad. There's foot-and-mouth disease in Hampshire, and the movement of cattle is prohibited. So of course it will be impossible to fetch the bull until the restrictions come off.'

'Oh!' Both Holly and Roy looked like deflated balloons.

'However, the ban is due to be lifted – let me see, what's the date of this – eleven days from yesterday. You'll need at least that time to get the horses fit for such a long journey, so you couldn't start for nearly a fortnight in any case. You'll just have to keep your fingers crossed against any more outbreaks of foot-and-mouth.'

To help pass the awful time of waiting they met Rebecca, and went for some long rides to get the horses fit. When they met Baynard they found that her reports of his height were very little exaggerated; he really was astonishingly tall, and Rebecca with her short legs seemed perched on him like a monkey on a stick. He wore an air of judge-like calm, and in spite of his gingery colouring was well mannered, which was lucky for Rebecca, who otherwise would have had little control.

Sarah fell for the handsome chestnut straight away, greeted him with seductive whickers and eyes shining with admiration. Her faithlessness enraged old Kelly, who lay back his ears, bared his long teeth, and waggled his head at Baynard, and Baynard, despite his superior size, took good care to keep out of the old cob's reach.

'I hope they get used to each other before they have to go in the box,' remarked Rebecca.

'Have you done anything about your luggage yet?' asked Roy. 'We've tried saddle-bags, but they weren't much good because they banged up and down when the horses trotted and cantered. I'm going to take a rucksack.'

'I tried carrying a rucksack, but it made my shoulders ache after a few minutes,' said Holly.

'I experimented with saddle-bags too,' said Rebecca. 'And I found that I couldn't mount at all because the near-side one got so in the way. Then I had a brainwave. I managed to get all my things into one of those long waterproof knitting bags with a zip, and strapped it to the front dees of the saddle where I can keep my eye on it.'

'How much can you get in a knitting bag?' asked Holly.

'Oh, just a spare shirt, washing things and pyjamas, a thin jersey, and a few other oddments. We shall start off in clean clothes, so one change ought to do.'

'Roy and I are going to share most things except pyjamas.'

'And toothbrushes in case of measles. We're sharing Sarah's and Kelly's brush too.'

'Not between yourselves!'

'We did think of that, but a dandy brush would be rather scratchy for our heads.'

'I don't suppose it's much good making too many preparations,' said Roy with sudden gloom. 'There are several days yet before the foot-and-mouth ban comes off.'

'Yes, anything might happen in that time,' agreed Holly.

Her remark was partly prophetic. When she and Roy got back that day they saw the hind quarters of a fat flea-bitten grey pony protruding through the gate.

'Why, it's Clive ridden over to see us,' said Roy, with a nonchalance that did not ring quite true.

Holly shot him a meaning look. She had purposely kept from saying any more about Roy's unfortunate invitation in the hope that nothing more would come of it, but this visit was ominous. They found Clive holding his pony, Alaska, and looking rather embarrassed while Mr Granger read a letter with a puzzled frown.

'Hi, you,' said the latter as they rode in, 'perhaps you can throw some light on this.'

He handed the letter to Roy, who had dismounted with a casual:

'Oh, hallo, Clive.'

'Hallo!' said Clive bleakly.

Holly read the letter over her brother's arm.

Dear Mr Granger,

It was so kind of you to invite Clive to go on a riding holiday with your children. There's nothing he would enjoy more, and it would do his pony such a lot of good because it doesn't get nearly enough exercise. Would you be so good as to let me know which day they start and what luggage Clive should take? As they are staying at youth hostels we have already made him a member. Would a primus stove be useful?

Yours sincerely,
Celia Prestwick

'I thought it would be all right for Clive to come along with us,' said Roy, returning the letter. 'But I don't see how we can carry a primus on horseback, do you?'

'When you issued the invitation did you stop to think what the Fowles might say to having their house turned into an hotel?'

'There you are, what did I tell you!' hissed Holly.

Roy's discomfort began to show, while poor Clive, who

was a sensitive boy, hardly knew which way to look. Meanwhile
Alaska was pawing the yard and splashing them all with mud.

'Look here, Clive,' said Mr Granger, 'your pony's getting very
restive. I think you'd better be riding along. Thank your mother
for her note, and tell her I shall be writing shortly.'

He held the bridle while Clive scrambled on, only too glad to
be going, and Alaska bore him out of the yard at a bouncing
trot.

'I'm sorry, but I did forget about staying the night at the
Fowles',' acknowledged Roy.

'You've certainly put me in a most awkward position,' said
their father. 'If it were not for disappointing Rebecca I'd call
the whole thing off. I shall have to phone up Fowle tonight and
see what he says about it before writing to Mrs Prestwick. I'm
really annoyed.'

Roy's disgrace was not improved by Holly, who could not
keep from harping on the possibility of the Fowles refusing to
put up any of them when they heard what had happened.

'Oh, very well, I was an idiot, and I'm sorry!' exclaimed Roy
at last. 'But you've done even sillier things in your time, and
you will do again.'

However, recriminations were forgotten when, after telephoning that evening, Mr Granger said:

'It's more than you deserve, but the Fowles have turned up
trumps. They're quite willing to put Clive up too.'

'Thank heavens for that!' exclaimed Roy, and Holly heaved
a great sigh of relief.

'And another thing,' went on Mr Granger, 'they made a mistake about the date of the foot-and-mouth ban. It comes off
tomorrow, so we can go down any time we like. I'll ring up
Poulter about his truck before anything else crops up; I suppose
I'd better ring up Mrs Prestwick, too, while I'm about it.'

Everything seemed to be happening at once, and when they
learnt that the truck had been booked for only three days ahead,
Holly and Roy completed their preparations at top speed.
Rebecca had to be consulted, and adjustments made to the
saddlery as well as the care of their live-stock to be considered.

The ferrets, rabbits, and Holly's goat were entrusted to Cecil, who was given many complicated instructions on their welfare. Their mother undertook to feed the Muscovy ducks and to keep an eye on Jacko, the jackdaw Roy had reared from a nestling.

Holly went into Ashford and bought herself a knitting bag, the biggest she could get. It was of shiny blue plastic adorned with yellow and pink rose-buds, and Roy declared that it was enough to make any horse except Kelly bolt with shame. He himself stuck to the rucksack, even though it bumped his back while cantering.

Sarah and Kelly, of course, came in for a lot of extra grooming. They had new shoes all round, their bridles soaped, and their bits and stirrup-irons brightly polished. The nosebands were removed so that headstalls could be worn under the bridles, and both had new white ropes for the occasion.

When Rebecca was told about the addition of Clive to the party she did not at first appear unduly concerned.

'How old is he?'

'Oh, about eleven, I should think,' replied Roy.

'Lor', quite a babe!'

'But he's pretty intelligent for his age. He won't be any trouble, you see.'

'But I bet Alaska will,' said Holly darkly.

'Alaska, is that where he comes from?'

'No, it's his pony. She's awfully hot, and does practically what she likes with him.'

'Look here, I hope I'm not expected to be responsible for the pair of 'em? Tell his mother they come at owner's risk!'

The day before they were due to start fate dealt Holly a cruel blow. Early that morning while she was stirring the porridge Joshua came to the kitchen door with the important air of one bearing evil tidings.

'Cecil will need to take the milk to the station with the tractor.'

'Whatever for?' asked Mr Granger, who was putting on his boots, and Holly's heart gave a lurch.

'Ould cob's lame.'

'No!' she screamed, abandoning the porridge.

'He is and all,' said Joshua delightedly. 'Lame as an ould sojer with a wooden leg.'

The news ran through the house, and the whole family came out to the yard where Kelly stood with his station-going harness hanging loosely upon him. His expression was one of mixed defiance and self-pity.

'See!' said Joshua, leading him a step forward.

Kelly floundered. No further trial was necessary to proclaim how very dead was his lameness.

'P'r'aps the blacksmith drew the clints too tight yesterday,' suggested Roy.

Their father, who was feeling the leg, shook his head.

'He's strained something; it's hot and swollen.'

'Oh dear, oh dear!' cried Mrs Granger, screwing up the oven cloth which happened to be in her hand. 'What about tomorrow?'

Poor Holly said never a word. Struck dumb by the calamity she could only stroke Kelly's drooping neck.

'Get him into the stable and bathe his leg with cold water,' said Mr Granger. 'I'll see if I can get on to the vet.'

Kelly cheered up at the idea of going into the stable, where there was a chance of some corn, and hobbled in fairly briskly. Roy took the harness off, while Holly fetched a pail of cold water, and her own sponge, and still in stricken silence bathed the swollen leg. Not even the smell of burnt porridge coming from the kitchen roused her from brooding despair. It was late morning before the vet got round to Haffeneys.

'He's strained it pretty badly,' he said after a short examination. 'Probably in a rabbit hole. I'll give you a tin of kaolin poultice which should bring the swelling down quite soon, but you'll have to rest him for a while.'

Roy put the question that Holly feared to ask:

'How long before he can be ridden?'

'You'll have to see how he goes on. Several weeks, I should say.'

'But we're starting on a riding tour tomorrow!' Holly found her voice at last.

'A riding tour, eh? I'm afraid this old chap won't be going. You'll have to find another mount.'

It was all very well for Mr Blackie to talk airily of finding another mount, but the Grangers knew perfectly well that there was no one in the district with a horse fit enough to start right away on a long tour. Rebecca had been lucky to get Baynard, but then that had been arranged some time before.

These points came up at a family conclave held in the stable after the vet had gone.

'Do you think the riding school would let Holly have a horse?' asked Mrs Granger.

'At a cost!' grunted Mr Granger, who was applying the poultice to Kelly's leg while Roy held the halter and Holly the bandage. 'And you know what their horses are like – half dying on their legs.'

'You'll have to ride home on the bull, Miss Holly,' croaked Joshua, who only made jokes when no one else was in the mood for them. 'Kelly's getting past them junketings, anyhow.'

'You'll just have to go without me,' said Holly, struggling to keep back the tears.

'Don't be a coon!' said Roy. 'We'll put it off till the summer hols.'

'But there won't be another chance of getting down to the New Forest,' Mr Granger pointed out.

'And Rebecca wouldn't be able to go then,' added Mrs Granger.

'And then there's Clive; don't forget you've invited him,' said Holly, unable to resist the dig.

'Oh, devil take Clive!'

Mr Granger finished Kelly's leg, and rose with an extra loud grunt.

'The truck's coming at eight tomorrow,' he said. 'Go on getting ready as if nothing had happened, and in the meantime I'll have to think of something.'

A ray of light pierced Holly's despair. When her father spoke of having to think of something it usually meant he had already done the thinking, and it only remained to put it into action.

Rebecca and Baynard arrived that evening, for they were staying the night in order to be ready for the early start on the morrow. The cheerful chatter as she and Roy ragged each other over their possible adventures rang very hollowly upon Holly's ears. She crept out to the stables in the twilight where Kelly stood resting his bandaged leg. His head hung despondently and his long lower lip trembled as he turned to greet her. Holly shed some tears in his earth-smelling mane, and fetched him a handful of illicit calf nuts which caused him to brighten immediately. Wiping her eyes on the back of her hand she returned to the house, where the lamps were shining out. Supper was being laid in the kitchen. At the end of the scrubbed table her mother sliced a loaf while Rebecca helped to make sandwiches for the journey tomorrow. There was a batch of freshly baked sausage-rolls to be packed, a cherry cake, and a row of hard-boiled eggs.

'Where's daddy?' Holly asked, hoping to hear that he had gone out on some business that might be connected with a horse.

'Doing accounts. Run in and tell him supper's ready.'

However, Mr Granger himself came in at that moment. He was smiling broadly.

'I daren't think what my telephone bill's going to be this quarter.'

'You've been phoning the Fowles again?'

'Right first time.'

'N-not to say we're not coming after all?'

'Wrong this time. I told Fowle the old cob had gone lame at the last minute, and asked if there were any likely horses or ponies down his way, and he said: "You've come to the right place, we've a whole forest swarming in 'em." '

'But wouldn't they be too wild?' broke in Mrs Granger.

'Of course he was only joking. But he did happen to know of one or two suitable ones from which we can choose when we get there.'

'But if I ride one home from there how shall we send it back again?' asked Holly in bewilderment.

'Oh, we couldn't send it back.'

They all stared at this.

'I've been thinking it over, you see,' said Mr Granger, sitting down to the table, and thoroughly enjoying the sensation he was causing, 'and I came to the conclusion that the cost of hiring a horse would come to nearly a quarter of its actual worth with nothing to show in the end. It's time Holly had something of her own a bit younger than old Kelly, who must be twenty if he's a day. So if we can find a reasonably priced animal down there it would be a good chance to buy one.'

This was rather more than Holly could take in straight away. Indeed, her first thought was one of alarm.

'What will happen to Kelly if we get another?'

'He'll go on taking the milk when his leg's cured. You needn't worry about him; he's too much of an institution to be got rid of.'

Reassured on this point, Holly's imagination took wing at the prospect of having a horse entirely of her own; perhaps it would be able to jump, and at least it would not have preconceived ideas about gymkhana events; a horse that could go hunting and not get blown after the first sharp run, who did not stumble in ruts or mind trotting downhill; and, above all, a horse on which to ride through the New Forest and all the unexplored country between it and Romney Marsh.

While this went on in Holly's mind hardly a word escaped through her mouth, which was mechanically occupied in eating her supper. The others all had plenty to say on the subject. Roy wanted to buy a wild pony out of a herd and break it in on the journey, but Rebecca pointed out that being both unfit and unshod the colt would be broken in more senses than one long before they got home.

'And so would Holly too,' exclaimed her mother. 'I hope to goodness you get one that's quiet and reliable.'

'Not too quiet,' said Mr Granger. 'She should be able to manage one with a little life in it. What do you say, Holly?'

'It simply must have a long tail,' said Holly inadequately.

'Just like a girl!' scoffed Roy. 'Conformation and soundness are the first things you should think of.'

'The tail is part of its conformation,' retorted Holly, sufficiently restored to normal to embark on a long argument.

But here Mrs Granger interfered.

'Get on with your suppers so that we can get washed up. It's early bed for all tonight if you want to be off in good time tomorrow.'

3

Mechanized transport

DAYLIGHT had not long chased the shadows westward across the Marsh when Haffeneys began to stir. Holly had slept fitfully, for each time she closed her eyes a procession of horses had passed before them. One of them was to be hers, but as it was twilight and they were all cantering it was impossible to see any of them clearly, and at last she fell into a real sleep from sheer exhaustion. Sunlight was throwing the lattice-work of the window in a shadow pattern on the opposite wall when her father tapped on her door.

Rebecca was awake but not yet stirring.

'I bet the horses had a good roll last night just to make more work this morning,' she yawned.

'Well, better get moving then!' Holly said, dashing into Roy's room to find he had started to dress and then fallen back on his bed again.

'Why can't we start at a civilized hour?' he mumbled when she shook him.

'Because we've got a long, long way to go!' trilled Holly, now as sprightly as a linnet.

'Sarah and Baynard looked slightly surprised at being caught in so early. They were taken into the stables for their final groom, and the dust motes rose and hung in the slanting bars of sunlight. Holly helped Rebecca with Baynard, standing on a box to brush his back while Kelly watched over the partition with his ears laid back.

A clinking of shoes against loose stones announced the arrival of Clive and Alaska. He had been told to come to breakfast, and he must have risen even earlier than the others, for he had seven miles to ride, and Alaska was beautifully groomed and did not even show a grass stain on her legs. His luggage was not so successful looking, being packed in a school satchel and fixed to the offside of the saddle, where it bumped on the pony's flank, while a mackintosh was strapped rather untidily to the front dees. His thin face was flushed and his eyes bright with excitement.

'Heavens, he *is* a kid!' exclaimed Rebecca, when she first caught sight of him. 'As you say, Holly, it's the pony that controls him half the time.'

'Oh, I expect Alaska will settle down; he said she only needed exercise,' said Roy hopefully. 'Hallo, Clive! Bring Alaska in and tie her up.'

Clive removed Alaska's double bridle after a struggle and tied her up to the ring in one of the stalls.

'She's not very used to being tied up.'

Alaska underlined this statement by pawing the floor and rooting up a loose brick. Roy brought her an armful of hay, but she tossed it out of the manger and trampled on it.

The breakfast bell was ringing and they hurried indoors. Knocks and bangs could be heard coming from the stable, and Clive ate very little of the food pressed on him by Mrs Granger.

'How does that pony of yours load, Clive?' asked Mr Granger.

'I d-don't know.'

'The truck's just turning in at the gate,' announced Cecil, coming to the kitchen door.

There was no thought of any more breakfast. They jumped up and started to carry out their belongings. An odd assortment they looked when heaped on the churn rack: knitting bags and Roy's rucksack, a basket with the lunch, two tall thermos flasks, saddles and bridles, two cockerels – 'Fowls for the Fowles,' said Roy, tossing them on the heap – and Mr Granger's old leather suitcase with a ticket marked 'Waterloo' still sticking to it.

Tim Poulter, the owner and driver of the box, nodded to them and began to let down the ramps with the aid of Cecil. Usually by this hour the farm men were out working, but this morning they had all found something to do round the yard. When the ramps were down the wooden inner gates were opened out to form wings. Clean straw gleamed in the dusky interior, and Tim spread some of this up the slatted ramps.

'Let's have the luggage in first,' he said, opening a little door in the side just behind the cab.

They stowed away the goods under a kind of bench, hung up some nets of hay, and then went to fetch the horses. Alaska had knocked several more bricks out of the floor and pulled the ring clean out of the manger. As the others were led out Kelly whickered dolefully. Holly comforted him with some oats and rubbed his broad brow.

'Josh is going to see to your leg, he's wizard with cures, and mummy will see that you get your bit of bread every day.'

Baynard ascended the ramp with a fine appearance of a horse accustomed to travel, and Sarah, although she snuffed suspiciously, was too eager to get to his side to jib. It was now Alaska's turn to climb in. At present she was revolving round Clive, and spinning him, too, like a top on the halter rope.

'You'd better let me take her,' said Mr Granger.

Alaska promptly struck out with a front hoof and caught Mr Granger a glancing blow on the shin. He gasped with pain, and seizing the rope up short with a vindictive jerk, hurried her towards the ramp. She put one hoof on the edge and then shot backwards as if it were red hot, dragging the thirteen-stone Mr Granger with her. Then began the battle. First she was coaxed with corn, patted, and soothed, then she was shooed, smacked, and threatened with a whip, but each time she slewed to one side or the other. They tried backing her in, and they tried blindfolding her, and at last they fetched a wagon rope, put it round her quarters, and all hauled upon it until she kicked herself free.

The mare grew wilder and wilder, and Clive stood by clenching his fists, while the tears ran down his face. Joshua's language reached a new pitch of velocity when he got his foot trodden on, and Bert, the pessimist, prophesied failure from the start; even Cecil's powers of invention failed him. Holly and

Rebecca, who had risked leaving the two horses tied up in the truck, anxiously marked the passing minutes. Only Tim remained imperturbable, remarking cheerfully between each fresh attempt:

'Never failed to get one loaded yet.'

'Well, I hate being beaten,' said Mr Granger, rubbing his leg tenderly, 'but if we don't get off soon we shan't be settled in by dusk. Shall we have one more turn with the rope?'

'No, no!' burst out Clive. 'Please don't! I'm sure she'll break her leg. I'd rather stay behind.'

'A dose of lead and a crane is what she wants,' said Joshua crudely.

'Never been beaten yet,' said Tim, glancing for inspiration round the yard.

His eyes fell upon a heap of sand and fine shingle left by the builders after repairing the cowshed. Picking up the bucket, which they had used at the beginning to entice the mare with oats, he filled it from the heap while the others watched with curiosity.

'Now, young man,' he said to Clive, 'seeing you're the one she knows, just lead her quietly up to the ramp, and you others be ready to shut the gates the moment she's in.'

The others smiled wearily at this display of optimism, but got ready. Bristling with suspicion Alaska went with Clive to the edge of the ramp. Before she could dash back Tim, who was coming softly behind, began to pelt her hind quarters with the sand and shingle. She swung to and fro, trying to escape the irritating shower, then bolted up into the truck, nearly knocking Clive over in her hurry to get away from what she could not see. The wooden gates were clamped together and the ramps heaved into place.

'Whew!' exclaimed Mr Granger, brushing down his rumpled clothes, flecked with white hairs, 'why on earth didn't you try that at first, Tim?'

' 'Twas something a bloke once told me, only I never thought of it again till I spotted that heap,' said Tim placidly.

After that no more time was lost in getting away. The engine started, final hasty farewells were taken of Mrs Granger, who had been witnessing the battle from the doorstep, and the travellers scrambled into their places, Mr Granger beside Tim and the others on the bench inside facing the horses.

The truck eased forward out of the yard, swung slowly round on to the road beside the canal, and then with gathering speed set off on its long journey westwards.

At first the horses travelled badly, staggering about like drunken creatures, but after a few miles they got their sea legs, and learnt the trick of leaning inwards at the corners. Baynard's great height added to his difficulties, for the tips of his ears brushed the roof and quite destroyed his serenity for a while. Sarah, foreseeing a rival in Alaska, tossed her head and snapped at the grey. But once in the truck Alaska had completely changed. Wedged back in the corner, well out of Sarah's reach, she managed to prop herself on three legs, and with her head supported on the taut rope fell into a doze.

'Why, all that commotion was just wilfulness!' said Rebecca. 'She's not a bit frightened of the truck really.'

Clive seemed to have lost interest in his pony. He knelt on the bench with his face pressed to one of the ventilator slits as if absorbed in the countryside. From time to time the others peered through the slits to see how they were getting on. The truck, although the rattle and roar gave the impression of speed, rarely exceeded twenty miles an hour, and it seemed a long time before they entered unfamiliar country. Then suddenly Holly cried:

'Look, the downs!'

The bored horses pricked their ears as the others crowded to her side.

'Yes, they're the downs right enough,' confirmed Roy. 'We may be riding along them soon.'

'Not too soon, I hope. We've got to get to the New Forest yet.'

All this time Clive had not said a word. Thinking that he might still be feeling shy over the way Alaska had delayed them Roy said kindly:

'We're getting on fine, Clive. I don't think we'll be late after all.'

Clive did not reply, but turned towards them a greenish-white face, with drops of sweat standing on the forehead.

'Good heavens, do you feel sick?'

He nodded desperately.

'I'm not much good at travelling, specially going backwards.'

'Hi, stop the truck!' cried Rebecca, thumping on the back of the cab.

As the truck came to a standstill the horses looked about hopefully, thinking it was they who were going to get out. Clive was bundled out on to the roadside. When he came back he looked a better colour, and Rebecca poured him out some tea from one of the flasks, and made him swallow it along with two aspirins.

'That should settle you,' she said rather ominously.

'I'm surprised you're not all sick in here,' said Mr Granger, putting his head in through the door.

Although the others had not noticed anything amiss before, since sniffing the fresh air they agreed that it was a bit thick inside.

'The sun's getting stronger,' said Tim, also coming round to investigate. 'It's making the horses sweat. You can have this door open if I tie it back with a bit of rope.'

'You'd better come in front with us, Clive,' said Mr. Granger.

Just before the outskirts of Southampton they pulled up again to eat their lunch beside the road and give Tim a rest from driving. While they ate they studied the maps and found that they were well over half-way to their destination.

'I hope we don't have to ride back along this awful main road,' said Rebecca.

'Of course not, we're going across country as much as we can,' said Roy. 'Those look like bridle-paths well to the north, and then we can dip down and get on to the South Downs.'

'You'll have to get on the main road at Totton, just by South-

ampton,' said Tim. 'There's no other bridge across the Test unless you go a long way round.'

In spite of the open door the atmosphere by mid afternoon
became very thick indeed. The sweating horses sighed and blew
through their nostrils showering their fellow travellers on the
bench in front of them. The heavy traffic round Southampton
slowed them down, but at last they reached an open heath rolling away to a distant belt of dark trees.

'Forest ponies!' exclaimed Roy, pointing out to the others
a herd of ponies, browns, chestnuts, and greys, grazing at a
little distance from the road.

They were really in the New Forest at last, and it was not
like anything they had seen before. The scarcity of hedges and
fences, the racks of fire-brooms beside the fir plantations, the
cows coming home unattended for milking, the pigs asleep at
the edge of the road, the notices warning motorists of ponies,
and the ponies themselves, sometimes pausing to suckle their
foals right in the way of the truck, all seemed quite contrary
to the orderliness of the fields and animals at home.

At last they got up on a very narrow, twisting, and bumpy
road. Despite all Tim's care the truck lurched alarmingly and
the tired horses could hardly keep their feet. It was a great
relief to all when, after a couple of jolts, as if they had gone
into a bomb crater, the truck came to a standstill and the engine
stopped.

'Well, here we are!' Mr Granger announced through the
hatch.

They lost no time in dropping down through the little
door, to be met by a welcome cool wind smelling of the sea and
pine-trees. They had come to rest in a farmyard, larger than
Haffeneys, and flanked on three sides by long brick buildings,
the roofs covered in yellow lichen. The house was set a little
way back among ilex-trees, and just opposite was a round iris-
fringed pond inhabited by variegated ducks. A herd of short-
horns filing out of the yard, urged on by a frenzied collie, took
Holly's thoughts straight home where, at about this time, their
own cows would be plodding back to the Marsh. Any twinges

of home-sickness were instantly forgotten as a tall figure came striding across the yard to greet them. They recognized Mr Fowle at once, even though he was not wearing his deer-stalker.

'So you've really made it! Well done, well done!' He wrung his old friend's arm nearly off and clapped the others on the shoulders. 'You must have set off at the crack of dawn. How many horses have you got in there?'

Not waiting to be told he peered through the door and nearly bumped noses with Baynard.

'This is a nice place you've got,' said Mr Granger, eyeing the buildings speculatively. 'That is, all but your road in!'

'Oh we don't call that a road! We call it the "test of friendship", because only those who really want to see us stick it out to the end. But you must be tired and hungry. We'll get the horses unboxed and fed, and then go in search of some tea.'

'Get the grey mare untied,' Tim told Clive. 'I guess she'll come out with a bit of a rush.'

His words were timely. Directly she heard the bolts released Alaska started to press back, and Clive only just freed the rope before she stampeded backwards down the ramp. Baynard and Sarah descended more circumspectly. They were taken into the cool stables and given food and water while Mr Fowle arranged for a man to show Tim his lodgings with the dairyman. Then they went into the house, where Mrs Fowle was waiting to give them tea. She was a gay, lively little woman, and as talkative as her husband, wanting to know all about their journey down. When Roy brought in the cockerels, looking rather dishevelled with wisps of hay among their feathers, she was delighted.

'You couldn't have brought me anything better! We've only laying hens left, and my husband won't hear of eating the drakes on the pond.'

Two burning questions kept Holly from enjoying her tea. One was, were they still in the New Forest, for what she had seen of the farm was not at all wild looking; the other, even more vital, where were the horses from which she was to choose her new mount? She took no interest in the talk of the grown-ups, stared round the room, and kicked her chair legs until her father gave her a disapproving look. Still Roy accepted another buttered scone, and Rebecca passed up her cup for the fourth time. Clive was the only one who finished early, but he seemed content to sit day-dreaming. At long last Mr Fowle stopped talking about old times and said:

'By the way, who is it wants a new pony?'

'Me!' cried Holly, upsetting her chair.

'Good! I've two lovely ones awaiting your inspection in the paddock. I had them sent along to save time. You'll be hard to please if one doesn't suit you.'

Holly had to curb her impatience for a little longer while Mr Fowle showed the others where to turn out the horses. He took a key from the porch and led them farther down the lane to a gate at the bottom.

'Why, there's the sea!' exclaimed Clive.

'Didn't you know we were by the sea? My land goes right down to the shore, and that hump across the way is the Isle of Wight. Your horses are getting sea air and a view that some people pay twenty pounds a week for on their holidays. We keep this gate padlocked because there's a footpath down to the beach, and it was always being left open. It's no joke when your cattle get out in the Forest.'

'Then this really is still the Forest?' asked Holly.

'Rather! There are about a hundred and fifty square miles of it, you know.'

'Can the horses get down to the sea?' asked Rebecca, with visions of Baynard swimming across to the Isle of Wight.

Mr Fowle assured her that there was a fence between them and the actual beach.

'It'll keep your horses in all right, though the Forest ponies manage to find their way in and out. Now we'll go and see about your pony, Holly.'

He took them to a small paddock behind the farm buildings, where two bay ponies grazed in company with some calves. Holly's heart fell, for the ponies were both smaller than any she had ridden for years. The larger of the pair was barely thirteen

and a half hands. She sought her father's face anxiously and
saw that he too looked dismayed; but it was Rebecca who said
bluntly:

'Won't they be too small for Holly?'

'Goodness, no!' said Mr Fowle reproachfully. 'You'd be surprised what Forest ponies can carry. Farmers, big chaps, ride
them, and even hunt on them. Catch them up, you boys, and
Holly can get her saddle and try them out.'

The ponies were caught and brought into the stables. No
fault could be found with their looks. They were both beautifully built, with intelligent heads and gentle manners.

'Look at their shoulders and quarters,' said Mr Fowle proudly.
'You could search the Forest and not better them.'

To Holly's relief Kelly's saddle was quite impossible on the
smaller pony, so it was transferred straight away to the larger,
whom it fitted a little better. Watched by the rest, she mounted
and rode up and down the farm lane. The pony moved so
lightly and softly that she hardly felt his steps, and neatly
skirted the pot-holes of his own accord. After the swing of
Kelly's big shoulders and his clopping stride she felt as if she
were riding on a rather small bicycle.

'Give him a canter,' said Mr Fowle, opening a gate into a
pasture field.

The pony whisked away into a canter. It was pleasantly
smooth, but his head seemed so low and she missed the feel of
a bigger horse's stride. When she dismounted she ricked her
ankle, forgetting how near the ground she was.

'Well, what do you think of him?' asked Mr Granger.

'Doesn't he go like a bird?' broke in Mr Fowle, glowing
with delight.

Poor Holly did not know how to reply. She knew she must
not offend Mr Fowle, who had done so much for them, and
there was no help forthcoming from her father, who was bend-
ing down feeling the pony's legs.

'He – he's lovely, of course,' she began diffidently, 'only I –
Mr Fowle gave her no chance to finish.

'I knew you'd fall for him! And he's a thundering good bargain; only a six-year-old with all his life before him. After you've ridden him for a day or two you'll swear he's the best pony you've ever been on.'

The ponies were put back in the paddock, and the two men went off to look round the farm before it grew dark.

'Whatever shall I do?' Holly burst out directly they had gone. 'It's a sweet pony, but miles and miles too small for me.'

'I expect he feels particularly small after Kelly,' said Roy.

'But her feet come below the girth now,' said Rebecca. 'In another year or so they'll touch the ground.'

'He's lower than Alaska, and not so broad, so he doesn't take you up that way,' said Clive.

'You'd better stand up for yourself, and insist that he's too small,' said Rebecca. 'You want a horse, not a pony.'

'But then what shall I ride home on? Daddy's got to start back first thing tomorrow, so there'll be no time to look for another one.'

They discussed the problem from all angles, but could find only two answers: either Holly must make the best of the small pony, or else give up the tour and go home with the truck the following morning. The thought of tamely going home was intolerable, and yet the fear of the little pony not being able to keep up with the others was almost as bad.

'Don't be silly; we won't forge on and leave you behind,' said Rebecca.

'But it's so awful being a drag and slowing everybody else down. And then if I do get the pony home all right what shall I do with him? I shall feel so silly having a new pony that looks too small right from the start.'

Holly's mind was still not made up by bedtime, although by their references to the riding tour the Fowles seemed to take it for granted that the pony was as good as hers.

4

Forest freedom

HOLLY woke next morning to the familiar throbbing of the engine which supplied current to the milking machine. This sound greeted her every morning at Haffeneys, and she stared in bewilderment at the sloping rafters of the attic and then at the bed opposite where Rebecca was still asleep. Recalling where she was she jumped up and ran to the dormer window. Through a frame of trees the Isle of Wight floated in a luminous haze distilled out of sea mist by the rising sun. A gap in the wild-rose hedge revealed the backs of the horses where they grazed in their seaside pastures: Baynard's chestnut form outlined in a thread of gold light, and the white parts of Sarah and Alaska looking like washing put out to bleach on a drying green.

This glimpse of the horses brought a wave of dejection over Holly, for it reminded her of her disappointment. She dressed hurriedly, waking Rebecca as she dragged on her shoes.

'It's early, isn't it?' yawned her cousin, groping for her watch. 'Oh, of course, we're in the New Forest. I had an awful thought I was in hospital and it was time to go on duty.'

'You needn't get up yet. I want to see if I can catch daddy alone.'

From the dining-room came the sounds of breakfast being laid, but she slipped unobserved through the deep porch and into the sunlight of the new day. It was absurd to feel anxious or dejected, with the sea and the island and, near at hand, the mighty Forest waiting to be explored. Her father was in the yard, talking to Tim about loading the young bull. Directly he had finished she burst out:

46

'Oh, daddy, what are we to do? The pony *is* too small for me, isn't he?'

'I think he's up to your weight,' began Mr Granger, but Holly cut him short with a gesture of despair.

'That means I must have him then. It wouldn't matter so much if we lived here, where apparently most people ride ponies. But the people at home wouldn't know that, and the trouble is I shall probably go on getting bigger.'

'I certainly don't want you to have him against your will,' said Mr Granger. 'It's a terribly awkward situation. There's only one thing I can suggest: I agree with Mr Fowle that the pony is a bargain, and I believe that if you rode him home we could easily sell him again for the same price. In fact if you kept him for a bit and rode him carefully so that he got a good name as a child's hunter or a gymkhana pony, we might even get more for him than we gave, and then buy you something a bit bigger.'

This idea of her father's cheered Holly up at once. Her imagination leaped ahead, thinking how she would train the Forest pony to be the best child's mount in the district. Trimmed up and with his mane plaited he might win a best pony class, or he might even turn out to be a wonderful show jumper. She was sure he would make a brilliant hunter, for she had already discovered his nimbleness.

'Well, are we going to settle it that way?' Her father interrupted her meditations.

She nodded eagerly, and he heaved a sigh of relief, for he had been blaming himself for leaving the finding of a mount for Holly so much to Mr Fowle.

Mr Granger and Tim departed directly after breakfast. The farm men had loaded Willoughby, the young bull, and he looked rather small and lonely in the big truck.

'See you again at Haffeneys, and in the meantime don't upset Joshua,' said Roy, as they closed the side door upon him.

Mr Granger issued last-minute instructions to the riders.

'Rest the horses in the middle of the day and loosen their girths – take the saddles right off, if you like. And make sure when you turn them out at night that the fields are safely fenced, or you'll be searching for them over half England. I think you should have enough money to see you through, but if you do run short phone up, and we can wire it to any post office for you to collect. But mind you,' he added, seeing a gleam of inspiration in Roy's eye, 'only for real emergencies. No sudden fancy for buying a camera or a new bridle and wiring to dad for the cash.'

Mr Fowle laughed at this.

'I see you know your children,' he said. 'But if they're keen on riding they'll keep out of the towns and won't see many shops.'

'And don't forget a few postcards home, just to keep your mother from imagining the worst.'

When the truck had swayed out of sight behind the great bank of greyish ilex-trees they knew they were really left to their own resources. Everything now depended on their horsemanship and skill as map-readers and path-finders, to cover the two hundred miles between them and Romney Marsh. They did not stand about considering this, but plunged straight away into preparations for the start. Putting their bags and packs ready in the stable, they went to fetch the horses from the pasture. Half-way down the lane they remembered the key, and Clive was sent back to fetch it from the porch. He returned breathless to announce that it was not there, and a look of consternation spread over Roy's face.

'You locked the gate yesterday; what did you do with the key?' asked Rebecca.

Shamefacedly he went through his pockets, confessing:

'I quite forgot to put it back, but it must be here.'

At the third search he turned out the linings, revealing a lot of useful articles, including the key to the harness-room at Haffeneys, but no key to the padlock on the gate.

'Let's try lifting the gate off its hinges.'

But long nails had been driven into the post just above the hinges to prevent just this very thing. They tugged at the chain and wriggled the padlock without avail, while the horses came up and watched their struggles with bland interest. Holly, who had got the Forest ponies in, met them coming back to the house to ask for a hacksaw. They had already promised to return the unwanted pony to its owner, which meant going a little out of their way to Buckler's Hard.

The hacksaw was blunt, and the steel loop of the padlock was equally strong, but after they had taken it in turns to saw, and become very hot and flushed, the chain at last slipped down from the gate with a welcome clank. By now the horses had removed themselves to the far side of the field and were gazing at the white sails of yachts on the Solent. By the time they were taken to the stables, saddled, and their luggage adjusted the morning was half gone. Baynard took the longest to get ready, for his saddle came too low on the wither, and he had to be reinforced by a numdah and some extra bits of felt provided by Rebecca, all of which needed careful arrangement while standing on extreme tiptoe.

At last they were ready to start, and Mr and Mrs Fowle assembled to see them off. Mr Fowle laughed over the affair of the padlock, and refused Roy's offer to pay for a new one.

'It's not the first time that's happened here,' he said. 'And, by the way, here's a little present for you that may come in useful on your travels.'

The present was a pocket compass, which thrilled Roy because it added a pioneering touch to their equipment.

As they rode out of the yard the ducks on the pond quacked and flapped their wings. They gave a final wave to Mr and Mrs Fowle, and then turned northwards up the rough lane. A light wind rippled the silken barley on either side, blew up the horses' manes, and swayed the young leaves in a merry mad way; their earlier frustration was forgotten, and the riders felt only the excitement of setting out into unknown countryside under the spell of approaching summer. Following Mr Fowle's directions they came out above Buckler's Hard, where slim painted boats lay at anchor in the estuary of the Beaulieu, and found the home of the pony's owner behind a hornbeam hedge. Only the wife was at home; she did not look very pleased at first.

'Have you brought them both back?' she asked. When they said no, only one, she cheered up. 'Though I wish it was the other one you were keeping. He's a little fiend for getting into my flower garden. It's high time all our ponies were turned back on the Forest.'

'How do you find them again?' asked Roy.

'Oh, they've got their brands, of course. And then the forest ranger usually knows where the different herds are.'

'What's the name of the pony we're keeping?' asked Holly, for the Fowles had been unable to tell her.

'Let me see, that would be Crumpet.'

'Crumpet? What a funny name!'

'I don't think much of it myself. T' other one's Muffin – they're both out of my husband's old mare, the one that had dark flecks over her back and was always known as Currant Bun.'

'I think I shall change his name,' said Holly, as they rode on their way. 'Crumpet sounds a bit comic.'

'Shortbread might be more suitable,' said Rebecca.

'There's no need to be clever just because you can't mount your horse without letting down the stirrup,' retorted Holly, touched on the raw.

So the pony remained Crumpet after that.

The first youth hostel on their route was at Burley, and Roy, who had taken charge of the maps, had been busy earlier looking up the best paths. But the way he now led them did not look as if it were going into Forest land at all – it was a green bridle-path, pleasant enough, but running through small woods and fields.

'This isn't a bit like the country we saw from the truck,' complained Holly. 'It's just like a bridle-path through the Weald of Kent.'

'Well, I really can't help it,' said Roy, who was getting tired of being blamed for everything that went wrong. 'It's the best way to Burley, and it says plainly on the map that it *is* the New Forest.'

'As long as it's off the hard road, I don't see that it matters much,' said Rebecca.

To Holly it mattered a great deal. She looked to see what Clive thought, but just then he was too busy trying to control the bouncing Alaska to enter into conversation. The school satchel bumped on her side and made her swish her tail. Crumpet trotted along with short nimble steps and ears intelligently pricked. His ears and a fluff of dark mane were nearly all Holly could see of him, for the knitting bag perched on his withers obscured the rest of his front.

'You're a perfect dear,' she addressed him, 'but so terribly near the ground. I do hope you'll be able to keep up with the others.'

'What did you say?' asked Rebecca.

'I was only talking to Crumpet. He has to take about three steps to Baynard's one; I hope he doesn't get too tired.'

'Oh, Forest ponies are said to be as hard as nails, and he'll be a perfect boon if we have many gates to open.'

This last remark of Rebecca's was soon proved, for there were several gates along the path. Baynard was ruled out from the start as a gate-opener, because Rebecca could not begin to reach down to the latch, Alaska would not stand still long enough, although she was good at shoving with her chest once it was unlatched, and whenever Roy bent down his rucksack tilted sharply over his head, nearly shooting him out of the saddle. Crumpet quickly learnt what to do, and stood like a rock while Holly fiddled with latches and chains.

Quite unexpectedly the path brought them out on a wide heath dotted with gorse bushes and grazed by little groups of wild ponies and cattle. Holly's heart, already on the upward trend because of Crumpet's cleverness, rose higher still.

'Oh, I am so glad we haven't missed all the wild part! Which way now, Roy?'

'Do you mind crossing a ford?' Roy asked them, looking up from the map which he had draped over Sarah's accommodating neck.

'Of course not,' said the others.

'As long as it's not too deep for Crumpet,' added Holly.

'Baynard can go first and test it.'

'Then this is our best way,' said Roy, folding up the map and
leading them down a sandy track into a valley.

Down in the valley trees grew for as far as they could see, and
right at the bottom the track was cut in two by a clear shallow
rivulet purling over its bright stones. Baynard sniffed the water,
put one hoof in and, finding the bottom firm, splashed majes-
tically across through six inches depth of water. Crumpet and
Sarah paused to drink. Suddenly Holly felt Crumpet going
down, and at the same time Clive, who was just behind,
shouted:

'Look out! He's going to roll.'

Holly jumped off in the water as Crumpet went down on his
side, and by beating him with the end of the rein got him to
his feet again before he could roll over on the saddle and her
luggage, and dragged him across to the opposite bank. Then
Roy, who had been sitting loosely on Sarah laughing at Holly's
plight, gave a yell as Sarah did exactly the same thing as Crumpet. He too was forced to step off in mid stream and tug her
across. Warned by their fate Clive drove Alaska hard at the
stream, so that she half leaped and half cantered across, splashing them all with the spray.

'I thought you knew better than to let them stand in the
water,' said Rebecca. 'Horses always roll in it, given the
chance.'

'How were we to know?' grumbled Holly. 'The dikes at
home are too muddy to stand in.'

The sandy path turned into greensward which soon widened
out on to a long green lawn closely nibbled by ponies. Great
oaks stood singly and in groups with thick ribbed grey boles,
their outstretched arms losing themselves in clouds of young
leaves coloured midway between bronze and gold. The hoof-
beats of the horses were muffled by the soft turf, which took
the print of iron shoes more sharply than those of the unshod
Forest ponies. The lawn branched out into other lawns,
equally green, and winding away into groves and woods where
the trees crowded more closely together.

Holly voiced everyone's opinion when she said simply:

'This is the place for lunch.'

Unbridling the horses and loosening their girths they teth-ered them where they could nibble the grass. Rebecca earmarked a fallen tree trunk to do duty as a mounting-block later, and in the meantime they sat upon it to eat their squashed sand-wiches. It had seemed such a pile when Mrs Fowle pressed the bags upon them that morning, and their pockets had been bulged out uncomfortably, but now that breakfast was sunk beyond memory the sandwiches barely filled the gap.

'That's one thing to remember: never turn down an offer of food however unhungry we feel at the time,' commented Roy.

Clive here rose sharply in the general esteem by producing two bars of chocolate and generously sharing them out.

They munched the chocolate gratefully while they looked about them.

'Just imagine Robin Hood and his Merry Men trooping down the forest glade,' said Rebecca, indulging in an unusual bit of fancy.

'William Rufus, you mean!' scoffed Roy.

'Well, what does it matter?'

'Robin Hood lived in Sherwood Forest.'

'I dare say he did, but I never liked Rufus because of his red hair.'

Soon after this they rode on deeper into the woods where the grass gave way to green bracken lapping the trees knee-deep. Not a breath of wind entered under the branches, and the un-curling fronds were poised as if in a frozen dance. It was very quiet, too, which made the squeaking of Baynard's saddle and Alaska's excited breathing much more noticeable. Then Roy, who was riding ahead with the map in his hand, reined in Sarah, halting the others like a line of railway trucks bumping into one another.

'Look! Look!'

For a breathless second the scene came to life as two deer crossed their path, and springing through the bracken vanished down the grey perspective of tree trunks. They were gone in a flash, and only the bracken swirling like green water in the wake of speed-boats marked their passage.

'He loved the tall deer as their father,' said Clive in the sing-song voice of one who quotes.

'Who did?'

'William Rufus, of course. That's why he made the New Forest for them, though only so that he could hunt them.'

'Fancy you remembering. But of course we did that period of history much longer ago.'

'And it's even longer when I did it; no wonder I got it mixed with Robin Hood,' said Rebecca, showing that she had been secretly annoyed over her mistake.

By late afternoon they reached the grassy stretch partly shaded by huge oaks which Roy said was Balmer Lawn. Here about a dozen mares with their foals and yearlings fed under the oaks. Bays like Crumpet predominated, but there were also a grey and a chestnut, and one of the mares had a skewbald foal. A pure black foal was fast asleep, stretched out flat like a scrap of velvet on the bright grass. The mares seemed quite fearless of the riders, who had paused to watch them, merely glancing up and then going on with their feeding. The older ponies had got their smooth summer coats, which showed up their brand marks, but the yearlings still had patches of bleached winter hair clinging to their bellies and thighs, which gave them a moth-eaten look. Two of the yearlings were having a mock battle, biting at each other's shoulders and necks and rearing higher and higher until at last the smaller one gave way and took refuge behind some mares. In doing so he disturbed the black foal, who rose awkwardly on his long legs, yawned and stretched like a cat, and trotted across to suck from his mother.

They all looked so tame that both Holly and Clive, who had dismounted, longed to stroke one of the foals. Without thinking they looped their reins on a bit of fence round an old lodge and walked towards the ponies. A tremor, like grasses swayed by a sudden breeze, passed through the herd. All the bright eyes of the mares were turned upon the intruders, and the foals sidled away behind them. A second chestnut, who had been grazing out of sight behind some bushes, now trotted towards them with head held high.

'This one must have been broken in, she's very friendly,' said Holly, turning to greet the newcomer.

The chestnut neighed like a distant train whistle and came resolutely on. Suddenly Roy cried:

'Look out, Hol! That's a stallion!'

The chestnut was the lord of the herd, and was intent, not on making friends, but on finding out what danger threatened his family. Although not much over thirteen hands high, he was a picture of masculine arrogance, his bright mane turning over silkily from his high-arched crest, his eyeballs rolling alarmingly, and the muscles rippling under his golden coat as he picked his feet high through the fern. Clive and Holly retreated from his path, but it was the other horses which had roused his anger. He whistled again, tossed his head defiantly at Baynard, who towered above him, and then made a rush at Crumpet by the fence. Holly shouted and waved her arms at him. With one accord the mares threw up their heads and wheeled away over the lawn with their foals and yearlings. The riding horses were equally startled by the noise and galloping, and Alaska, who had been fidgeting all the time, dashed backwards, snapped the rein, and galloped after the herd with the saddle-bag walloping madly against her side.

Roy and Rebecca rode off in pursuit with useless cries of 'Whoa there!' and 'Steady!' Holly ran to hold Crumpet, who was also on the verge of breaking loose, and Clive ran in the wake of the riders shouting Alaska's name. Meanwhile the stallion, seeing Alaska coming, decided that the plump grey mare would be a nice addition to his herd, and, neatly circling, drove her on with the others. They crossed the lawn and dashed out of sight through the trees.

Holly managed to mount Crumpet, whose agitation at being thus left by the others was understandable.

'Catch my stirrup!' she shouted as she overtook Clive. 'It'll help you along.'

Soon they met Rebecca cantering back.

'They look like going for miles. You'd better get up behind me, Clive. Roy has gone on to see which way they go.'

It was not easy for Clive to get up on Baynard, and Holly had to dismount again and make a back for him. Baynard's dignity was much impaired with two riders bobbing on his back. Clive was distraught.

'We shall never see Alaska again,' he kept repeating. 'I wish I hadn't come.'

The path the ponies had taken led out on to a hard road. On the other side they saw Roy standing still. He signalled to them to come slowly, and when they joined him said in a low voice:

'They're just down in the dip, moving quite slowly now. If we edge up to them we might be able to cut Alaska out.'

They rode cautiously down the track and saw the herd moving ahead of them at a walk. Alaska looked unhappy, for the mares resented her presence and kicked when she came near, while the stallion drove her on from behind. Directly the stallion saw the riders he neighed again and drove the herd on into a trot. The yearlings kicked up their heels as if enjoying the chase, but the mares called anxiously to their foals to keep near them. Alaska, with the stallion nipping her flank, bucked along on the edge of the herd.

'I don't see how we're ever going to get near them,' said Rebecca, her usually cheerful face troubled. 'There's nothing to stop them keeping on till dark, and then we shall lose them altogether.'

'I wish we had a lasso,' said Holly.

The others were too worried to point out that none of them knew how to use a lasso even if they had one. There was not a hedge or a fence in sight against which they might corner the ponies. What did turn up, however, was a man riding a brown pony at a rapid trot.

'Is that your grey?' he called.

They nodded vehemently.

'Then our best plan is to move them slowly along towards

Mrs Holland's place. They're mostly her mares, and there's just a chance we could drive them into her paddock.'

He was a tall spare man, and his long legs seemed to drape themselves round the stalwart little pony. A bundle of tools done up in sacking was roped across his back, and a coil of rope hung from his saddle bow.

'Is it far to this paddock?' asked Rebecca.

'Only a mile or so. We'll spread out in a minute. The main thing is to stop them breaking back towards Balmer, which is what the chestnut horse will try to make them do.'

The herd had dropped to a walk, and one or two of the young ones hung back to nibble at leaves, but the wary stallion hustled these on. The leading mares seemed to be making for some definite place, choosing the path without hesitation, while their foals trotted demurely at their sides. But the stallion was growing more restless and kept veering first to one side and then to the other with his eyes fixed on the pursuers. With a gesture of his arm the man indicated that it was time for the riders to spread out. They did so none too soon, for the stallion suddenly darted forward and drove the leading mares to the left. Roy urged the willing Sarah to a gallop, and headed them back on to their former path. Several times the stallion tried to turn the herd, but the riders were able to defeat his efforts, partly aided by the mares, who showed definite signs of wanting to press forward in defiance of their master.

A belt of pine-trees topped the rise of heathland, and as they drew nearer they saw the roofs of some buildings through the boles. The man motioned them towards him.

'I'm hoping someone will see them coming up the slope and open the gate for them,' he explained. 'So we'd better let them go slowly.'

Once again the herd dropped to a walk. As they wound up the track with the level rays of the setting sun shining on their backs and manes they made an attractive sight. But the four travellers were hardly able to appreciate this, with Alaska still loose and the lateness of the hour reminding them that they still had to find their night's lodgings.

'There's someone waving!' exclaimed Roy suddenly.

'That's right! It's Mrs Holland, and she's seen us.' And the man waved back. 'Now be careful in case they break away at the last minute.'

A fence ran along inside the fringe of pines, and in it was a gate that had been propped open, while a short fenced lane led up to it like the wings of a jump. The stallion made one last effort to turn the herd, but the old grey Forest mare, who had been in the lead all the time, disregarded him, and, calling to the others, trotted almost eagerly up to and through the gate. The others jostled close upon her heels. As they passed through, with Alaska and the stallion last, a figure in a long light dust-coat emerged from behind a tree and shut the gate on their tails.

'Alaska's safe!' cried Clive, struggling to dismount while Baynard was still on the move.

The person who had closed the gate turned to meet them. She was a tall lady, no longer young, with a weather-browned face and a blue felt hat pulled firmly down to hide every vestige of hair.

'I won't thank you for this little lot, Mr Blake,' she barked rather than spoke to the man. 'I've got a stable full of ponies now, and no one to help me. But I suppose these young people are in some kind of trouble, and you, as usual, turned up in the nick of time to the rescue.'

5

Jobs for all

THE ponies were now confined in a small paddock with high
wooden rails and, on one side, a row of thatched loose boxes
from which looked out a number of interested heads. Clive
immediately began to climb over the railing with the intention
of catching Alaska, but he was stopped by Mrs Holland.

'Wait a minute, wait a minute, young man,' she snapped.
'The mares don't know you, and the horse is in a bad mood. I'll
go in to them first, and then you can try to catch your pony.'

'I think she'll be glad to leave them; the mares aren't giving
her much of a time,' said the man referred to as Mr Blake. 'I
suppose you took a toss, sonny, and lost hold of her?'

Clive hung his head, knowing that he had committed a car-
dinal sin by tethering Alaska by the rein, and Holly kept quiet,
knowing that she too had helped to cause the catastrophe. They
were saved from explaining what had really happened by Mrs
Holland beckoning to Clive to be ready.

'All right, my girls, steady there!' She spoke to the mares
in a very different tone than she had used to the humans.

The mares knew her voice and pricked their ears, and the old
grey took a step forward and allowed her neck to be stroked.
The chestnut stallion had retired into the background at Mrs
Holland's approach, and stood snorting and tossing his head.
Alaska, glad to be free from his attentions, veered off by herself into a corner. Clive approached her, calling her name softly.
She whickered in answer and let him take hold of the trailing
rein. Plainly she had had quite enough of wild life, and followed him eagerly back to her domesticated friends.

'Lucky for you she got in with Mrs Holland's bunch and not

with some others,' said Mr Blake. 'Mrs Holland feeds her mares in the winter, so they're comparatively tame, but it's often a day's work for several riders to get in some of the ponies, and then they may escape in the end. A couple of nights bridled and girthed up wouldn't have done your pony much good.'

It seemed that travelling through the Forest was not at all the same thing as riding through the enclosed Weald, or even upon the Marsh. Although Roy had once lost Sarah on the Marsh for some time before cornering her in a sheep pen, there had been no real danger. They all now resolved to keep their wits about them and take no more risks. These solemn reflections were interrupted by Mrs Holland calling out to them to open the gate again to let the herd out.

'Take your horses out of the way and hold on tight to them!'

The stallion had never taken his eyes off the gate since entering the paddock. The moment it was opened he shot through it, and the obedient herd poured after him in a throng of waving manes and tails. They cantered away until they were clear of the trees, then quickly sobered down and plodded back along the track.

'I guess that's the shortest catching in they've ever known,' remarked Mr Blake.

'I didn't want them eating off my young grass for a moment longer than necessary,' replied Mrs Holland. 'I've too many saddle ponies to keep on it. Now what's the matter, little boy? Pony been kicked?'

'No, but my saddle-bag's gone,' said Clive faintly. 'The dees have pulled right out.'

'It must have caught in something coming through the first lot of trees,' said Rebecca. 'We should have seen it come off in the open.'

'That's a long way back,' said Holly. 'Was there anything valuable in it beside night things?'

'Yes, nearly all my money.'

'Oh, good heavens!'

'We'd better go back and look for it,' said Roy.

'But it'll soon be dark, and we haven't found our way to

the hostel yet, nor anywhere for the horses.' Rebecca reminded them.

'I shall be riding back that way,' said Mr Blake. 'The grey certainly hadn't a saddle-bag when I first saw her, so it would be coming through those trees right enough where she lost it. If I find it I'll hand it in to the police station at Brockenhurst. You don't want to get benighted if you're strangers here.'

Clive still wanted to go back and look for the saddle-bag himself, but the others persuaded him to accept Mr Blake's offer. 'You're jolly lucky to have Alaska safe without grizzling over a saddle-bag,' Holly told him.

'Please, how far is it to Burley?' Rebecca asked Mrs Holland.

'About six miles if you know the tracks. But you're not Burley people, and I've not seen those horses before.'

'No, we're on our way to the youth hostel.'

'Do you mean you're on a riding tour? Where from, and where to?'

'We started from Lymington this morning, and we're going home to Romney Marsh in Kent,' explained Holly, thinking how fine that sounded.

'And do you book accommodation along the way ahead?'

'Oh, no, we never thought of that.'

'We mightn't get to where we'd booked each night,' said Roy, adding with some point: 'You never know what may happen with horses.'

'I do think that is splendid!' broke out Mrs Holland with real admiration in her hitherto snappy voice. 'Personally, I'd like to know where my horse and I were going to land up each night, but maybe I wouldn't have minded forty years ago.'

'Well, we really ought to be pushing on,' said Rebecca, looking at her watch. 'Clive, have you thanked Mrs Holland properly for helping to catch Alaska?'

Mrs Holland brushed aside Clive's stumbling words, saying sharply:

'Not at all. What are you going to do with the horses at

Burley? I don't know any one there who could take them in
for you.'

'Oh dear!' said Holly. 'And they're more important than
us.'

'I know, I know.' Mrs Holland nodded her old blue hat in
approval of these sentiments. 'I'd take them in for you myself – I keep a small riding school, you see – but I'm just at my
wits' end to know how to get round. My resident pupil was
called off to look after her mother and won't be back until
tomorrow night, and this morning my sister twisted her knee –
an old weak point of hers – and is literally held by the leg. So
I have all the house and cooking, the riding ponies, and a certain amount of stock to see to single-handed. I'm behind as it
is, thanks to this little lot. Oh, I wasn't exactly blaming you,
but everything happens at once in this place.'

Holly, Roy, and Rebecca looked at each other inquiringly
during Mrs Holland's recital of her troubles, the same thought
occurring to them all. Clive, still worrying about his lost saddle-
bag and Alaska's broken rein, was the only one not to jump to
the obvious conclusion.

'Can't we stay and help you?' asked Rebecca. 'You see, we've
no fixed time-table, so an extra day in the Forest wouldn't
matter at all. We can all do stablework and housework, and
I'm not too bad a cook.'

'And we can look after stock and ponies, can't we, Clive?'
said Roy.

'Oh, yes, rather,' said Clive, waking up to what was going
on.

Mrs Holland looked from one to another with dawning delight until her thin brown face broke into a wrinkled fan of
smiles.

'My dears, could you really? It would be a godsend. Your
horses would have to be in at night, because I need the pad-
docks for the ponies, but I've plenty of hay, and they could
go out during some of the day. Your help would save me having to put off some of my rides tomorrow, and if you'll stay
and do some jobs now I'll give you supper and run you into

Burley afterwards in my old van. I'd love to have you; I see you're a crowd after my own heart!'

They all agreed to this plan at once, and Mrs Holland told them to hold their horses while she let the ponies out of the stables. There was a little yard fenced off in front of the boxes, and when the gate of this was opened the riding ponies trotted eagerly out into the paddock. They cantered round for a few minutes like a pack of puppies before nibbling the short grass greedily. All the ponies were built on the same lines as Crumpet, two dark bays and a light one, a roan, a black, and a liver chestnut, and they made a pretty collection against the background of tawny-barked pine-trees.

Mrs Holland waved to them to bring in the horses, but when she saw Baynard at close quarters she shook her head in dismay.

'What a whopper! He'll have the roof off if we put him in one of these pony boxes. He'll have to go in the garage; it's not the first time my poor old van has had to make room for a horse.'

Sarah, Alaska, and Crumpet were accommodated in three of the little boxes with blue doors, and Mrs Holland showed their owners where to get hay, water, and dried fern for their bedding. Then she conducted Baynard to the garage, which was next to the thatched bungalow. It proved to be a simple matter of moving a few petrol tins and a jack and putting up some bars to transform this into quite a roomy box capable of housing Baynard. His ears were a trifle near the rafters, but no worse than when he travelled down in the truck. When the horses were made comfortable Mrs Holland said:

'Now I'll organize my labour gang. Most of the stable-work will be tomorrow when we get the ponies ready; in the meanwhile can anybody milk?'

'Me!' answered Roy and Holly, both having served an exacting apprenticeship under Joshua before the dairy was electrified.

'Well, as Bessie is used to women it had better be Holly. There are pigs and poultry to feed too, and perhaps you boys would cut the chaff ready for the midday feed tomorrow, as the ponies don't go out to graze until the evening. The tack we'll do after supper when my sister can help, and talking of supper, perhaps you, Rebecca, would have a shot at cooking the eggs and bacon.'

They were organized in no time. Mrs Holland produced the milking pail and took Holly to the little cowshed, which joined on to the stabling and was thatched like the rest. Two cows waited outside on the heath for the gate to be opened. They were Channel Islanders, with soft, russet-tinted coats and huge dark eyes.

'Do they live out in the Forest all the time?' asked Holly.

'Well, I've been leaving them in the paddock at night of late because Bertha is expecting a calf soon, another of my worries. Come on, girls, kup, kup, kup!'

The two little cows stepped neatly into the shed and started in on their nuts while Holly put the chains round their lowered heads. Remembering the cold, much-swilled cement floors, tubular iron partitions, and lengths of rubber tubing at home, she thought how Joshua would disapprove of this humble but cosy outfit. When the milking was finished the cows were turned into another paddock at the back, in company with a couple of mares and foals.

'Why are these mares kept in?' Holly asked, as Mrs Holland helped her put up the bars.

'Because they're rather special. I'm showing them in the mare and foal classes at the show, so I want to keep them under my eye and handle them a bit.'

'Oh, I do hope they win! But aren't they rather different from each other?'

'Quite right. The dark mare, Trudy, is what I consider to be the perfect type of riding pony. The other one, Moss, with the chestnut foal, is what we call a utility pony, the sort that commoners can use in harness as well as for riding. That pony Mr Blake was riding is a very good example of one, a bit heavier than the purely riding ponies but very active. That's a nice type of pony you were riding. Got him in the Beaulieu district, didn't you?'

'Why, however did you know?'

'By his tail notch, of course.'

'Well, I noticed he had a chunk cut out, but I didn't know it meant anything.'

'Very much it does. Differently placed notches stand for different districts. You'll learn a few things about the Forest if you stay here long enough.'

With so many willing hands the work about the little steading was soon done, and as dusk was falling they were called into the bungalow, from which drifted the pleasing smell of frying. In the small crowded living-room, its walls lined with photographs and pictures of ponies, Rebecca was setting out heaped-up plates of egg, bacon, and fried potatoes round the table. Mrs Holland's sister, whom she introduced to them as Miss Fry, was sitting on a couch with her leg propped before her. She was younger and prettier than Mrs Holland, with reddish hair and a few freckles, and she showed great excitement over the visitors.

'I've been dying to meet you all! It *is* good of you to stay and help us out, and please tell me all about your tour and the horses. Rebecca has told me how you came down in a truck, but then the bacon started to burn and she had to break off.'

'Eat first!' commanded Mrs Holland, who had at last taken off her blue hat and dust-coat, revealing a close-cropped grey head and an amazing number of woollen jumpers and cardigans. 'We can talk while we're cleaning tack.'

Although they were aching with hunger, the four visitors did not like to seem too greedy at first, until their hostesses assured them that the larder was well stocked with home-bred bacon and eggs.

'Go on, eat up, eat up! We shall get our dividends out of you all right.'

After that they had no compunction over a second helping, topped up with scones, butter, and jam and tea from an enormous blue pot.

After supper they put newspaper on the table and brought in six sets of pony tack to be cleaned. None of them showed

much enthusiasm for tack-cleaning at home, but here it was like
a party, sitting round in the lamp-light swopping riding stories
while they soaped and polished. Mrs Holland insisted on brew-
ing up a steaming jug of cocoa with which to mark the end of
the task, and she also stitched Clive's broken rein with a natty
little tool which she said was the mainstay of the riding school.

'And isn't it time you phoned the police about your bag?'

Clive had been longing to do this for some time, but had
been too shy to ask if he might use her telephone. In fact the
worry over his bag had prevented him from saying very much
all the evening. When he returned to the room they knew by his
expression that all was well.

'Mr Blake did find it,' he announced radiantly. 'Oh, goody,
goody! It had my savings bank book as well as my money and
other things.'

'You never told us that!' exclaimed Rebecca.

'I just somehow couldn't mention it in case it was lost for
ever.'

'Well, we can pick it up on our way to Burley,' said Mrs
Holland. 'It's time I got the old van started up, or you won't
be down at the hostel before they close.'

Complicated things had to be done by torch-light to the
engine before the ancient green van decided to move. There
was only room for one in front, and the other three sat on some
sacks on the floor. The bumpy journey seemed long, but this
may have been due to the cautious driving of Mrs Holland.

'I won't take you right to the door of the hostel. Aren't they
rather fussy about people arriving under their own steam? I'll
drop you by the post office, and will look out for you there
again at half past eight tomorrow.'

When they went into the hostel the light made them blink
and they could hardly see to fill in the columns of the atten-
dance book presented to them by the warden. They paid their
small sums, ordered breakfast, and hired themselves a cotton
sleeping-bag apiece.

'Won't this be rather cold?' asked Holly, shivering.

Laughing, the warden told her that the bag was merely to

be used like a sheet, and that she would find plenty of blankets on the beds upstairs. It was all extremely simple, and no one seemed at all concerned over their grubby, dishevelled appearance or scanty luggage.

As it was nearly ten o'clock they decided to go straight to bed, although sounds of mirth coming from the common room indicated that other hostellers were still up and doing. However, when they parted from the boys and entered the women's dormitory, several recumbent forms showed Holly and Rebecca that they were not the first to think of bed. Rebecca complained a little of the closeness of the beds, her professional training having made hygiene something of a habit. But Holly, suddenly overcome by weariness after all that they had done that day, felt she could not be bothered over such small things as germs. She made her bed and fell into it, muttering sleepily:

'They'll all be blown away in the Forest tomorrow, so what's the odds?'

'All right, but I will have one window open,' insisted Rebecca.

The squeal of the frame and protesting grunt from the form in the next bed were the last things Holly knew of their first day's riding tour.

6

Riding with Mrs Holland

'WE do get some jobs when we go on riding tours,' said Rebecca.

It was early morning, and she and Holly had been detailed by the warden to sweep out their dormitory. There seemed to be a great deal of dust which was difficult to get up owing to the closeness of the beds to each other, and also to the fact that a number of other girls were busy folding their blankets and filling their packs. The sweepers did their task to the accompaniment of 'Excuse me,' 'Do you mind?' 'Oh, sorry!' 'Not at all,' 'Carry on with the good work!'

When they had secured what looked like a good catch of dust and rubbish they roamed the hostel looking for a dustbin, and so encountered Roy and Clive washing up the breakfast things along with some others.

'Well, it's very refreshing to see *the men* doing some housework,' remarked Holly gleefully.

In spite of having to do their share of chores, they agreed that there was nothing like staying in a hostel for friendliness and a free-and-easy way of life. There was a delightful adventuring atmosphere with so many people dressed for the road and gathered together with their packs, rucksacks, large boots, or bicycles.

Booking their beds for another night, and leaving their bags with the warden, they were out of the hostel in good time to meet Mrs Holland. Even so, the battered green van was already waiting outside the post office.

'It's all right, you're not late,' she greeted them as they started to run. 'I came in early to do one or two bits of shopping. Slept all right?'

'Like tops.'

'I've done the milking and fed the animals, so we can concentrate on the ponies,' she went on as they drove along the
winding road. 'We've got something of a reputation for smart-
ness, and I don't want to let the standard down if I can help
it. I've three small children to teach this morning, and a bunch
to take out for a two-hour ride this afternoon, older ones, of
course, so if you want to see a bit more of the Forest you can
come too.'

'Oh, we'd love to!'

'And it will be a good thing to exercise the horses as they've
been in all night,' added Roy.

'I should think that grey pony could certainly do with some.
Welsh bred, isn't she?'

'Yes, she's supposed to be a Welsh Mountain pony,' said
Clive. 'She never gets tired, you know.'

'I can quite believe that. I had to shut her top door last
night when I got back. She suddenly heard the other ponies
moving in the paddock and thought she'd like to join them.
In fact we had quite a night of it, because I forgot to tell my
sister that we'd put Baynard in the garage, and she woke me up
to tell me that someone was trying to start the van. I expect it
was old Baynard snoring.'

There was plenty to do when they got to the stables. Baynard, Sarah, Alaska, and Crumpet were all eager to get out and
taste the grass they could see from their doors, but first they
had to be tied up in the little yard while the boxes were mucked
out, the manure wheeled away, and the Forest ponies haltered
and led in. Grooming was quite a big job, for the ponies had all
rolled the evening before, but half an hour's intensive brushing
and rubbing brought their coats up bright and glossy again
and their tails and manes flowing out silkily. The ponies who
were to be ridden that morning were saddled and bridled and
put on pillar reins ready for the children's arrival. Mrs Holland
who, because there were not enough grooming tools to go
round, had retired into the bungalow to do a 'spot of housework', reappeared to supervise the saddling and bridling. She

had changed her dust-coat for a riding one in a small neat
check pattern, and the blue hat for one with a flatter crown
ornamented by a deer's hoof set on a silver pin.

'While I'm out with these two small ponies and old Gorse
would you like to try your hands at whitewashing their boxes?
I can lend you some old coats to put on and things for your
heads.'

Whitewashing was just Roy's forte. He seized eagerly upon
the bag of whitening, and insisted on doing all the mixing
himself. He had knocked up a couple of buckets of creamy
fluid by the time the first riders appeared, a little brother and
sister in velvet caps, much too big, and baggy jodhpurs asking
to be grown into. The little boy was mounted on Brocade, the
roan, and his sister had Shandy, one of the bays. Mrs Holland
rode an old chestnut mare which set off serenely with a pony
attached on either side by leading reins. When this cautious
cavalcade was out of sight the others rolled up their sleeves
and set to work. Flop, flop went the heavy brushes, accompanied
from time to time by exclamations as they splattered one another, and by injunctions from Roy to 'keep the wallop stirred'.
By the time Mrs Holland and her pupils came back the three
boxes were done, and smelled very clean and rather damp.

'A proper spring-clean that!' she said. 'These three ponies
will be all right in the yard during dinner. If we put them in
the boxes before they're dry they'll come out skewbalds this
afternoon.'

Dinner was cold ham and baked potatoes, followed, rather
surprisingly, by plum cake and a pot of tea.

'We never have time for real tea,' explained Miss Fry, 'so
we have it for pudding, which saves an awful lot of bother.
Where to this afternoon?'

'Have you chaps seen the Rufus Stone?' asked Mrs Holland.

'What's that, something you kiss?' inquired Rebecca.

'Well, you could kiss it if you had the urge, but I've an idea
you're thinking of the Blarney Stone. This one marks the spot
where William Rufus was killed while hunting. It's nothing to
look at, but it's a nice ride there, and just the right length.'

They were eight strong when they set out to view the Rufus Stone that afternoon. It took a little while for the visiting horses to settle down in company with the riding-school ponies. Baynard acted in a most peculiar manner, arching his neck, taking very high steps, and snorted loudly, much to Rebecca's discomfort.

'My, what a giant!' exclaimed a rosy-faced boy called Jock. 'He's the biggest horse I've ever seen that wasn't a cart-horse.'

The other two riders were an older boy, Martin, and a supercilious young lady called Miss Clegg. Miss Clegg was very taken by Sarah, and suddenly asked in a thin high voice:

'Can I ride the piebald horse?'

Roy was quite taken aback, but before he could answer Mrs Holland replied sharply:

'These four are visitors, and don't belong to me, and anyhow she's a mare and skewbald; how many more times must I explain the difference? You can ride Fern, who carries you very well.'

'But I'm tired of these small ponies.'

'Well, Fern's the tallest, too tall for a good Forest pony.'

Miss Clegg tossed her head, and mounted the biggest bay pony. From the way she kept looking at the others it was plain that she both envied and respected them for possessing their own mounts.

'I'd have one of my own if we had somewhere to keep it at home. A decent-sized horse,' she said with a withering look at Mrs Holland, which had no effect whatsoever.

'Don't you let her touch your mare,' said Mrs Holland in a low voice to Roy. 'That girl couldn't ride a decent horse, as she calls it, if she had one. She's nothing more than a passenger. Fortunately Fern has more sense in one ear than she's got in her whole body. Now the two boys are good sports and really devoted to the ponies, though Martin can be a little reckless at times.'

The party set off along a path leading through an enclosure of young firs. Alaska electrified them by dashing away at a canter with her tail high in the air. The astonished Forest ponies, who had been trained to walk the first mile out, were about to start forward after her, but a sharp word from Mrs Holland checked them. After a few bucks Clive managed to pull Alaska up and trotted her back.

'It was having so many others excited her. I think she thought it was a hunt,' he explained.

'And is that how you start off hunting?' said Mrs Holland, shaking her head. 'I'd go white instead of just grey if I had to be responsible for someone on a pony like that.'

'I think she's a beauty,' said Martin with shining eyes.

'I must say I do like a pony with a bit of go,' sighed Holly. 'Crumpet is terribly sweet, but he's just as ready to stop as he is to go.'

'What I call a well-trained pony,' commented Mrs Holland. 'Why do you want to sell him when you get home? He carries you perfectly.'

'But do you think he would get on all right hunting in the mud?'

'Well, if you have very deep going down your way it might tire him. But you should get a good price for him. There are plenty of ponies about, but very few really well-broken ones fit for children to ride.'

Holly was encouraged by this praise of Crumpet, and began to plan in her mind the type of horse she would buy if she sold him for a lot of money. Would she get enough to buy a thoroughbred? she wondered. A chestnut with a red mane and tail and white socks and a great turn of speed. If he were a good jumper, too, she would enter him for a point-to-point. She was just in the process of overtaking the rest of the field and making a brilliant dash up the straight to the winning post, when a scrap of whispered conversation brought her back to the present.

'I'm almost sure Bosky could beat her,' Martin was saying to Clive. 'Look, there's a place coming where we nearly always canter. We'll get in front and let them out.'

'All right,' replied Clive. 'But I warn you, once Alaska gets really going there's no holding her.'

It dawned upon Holly that a real race was being planned, and one of which Mrs Holland was certain to disapprove. The Forest ponies began to quicken their paces ready for the canter which they knew was coming over the stretch of heath beyond the enclosure. First they had to pass through a gate, and while Mrs Holland was shutting it behind them Clive and Martin, who was on the black pony, edged themselves to the front. Holly held her peace because she wanted to see the race.

'This is a nice safe track to canter along,' said the unsuspecting Mrs Holland. 'Shorten your reins, keep your heels down, and go at a nice collected pace.'

She had hardly finished these instructions when Alaska and Bosky were away amid a chorus of 'Ooohs!' from the other riders, and snorts of indignation from Baynard and Sarah.

'Hi, pull up!' shouted Mrs Holland. 'Steady him, Martin.'

It quickly became plain to all that neither rider was making the least effort to pull up, and were, instead, urging their ponies on. Mrs Holland's face was like a thundercloud.

'Keep behind me!' she ordered the rest of her band, and they lolloped along in her wake at a decorous canter while Alaska and Bosky became smaller and smaller, and at last passed out of sight round a belt of woodland.

When the others rounded the bend they found the two jockeys had been stopped by a high gate leading into the next enclosure. They had dismounted and were dubiously eyeing their ponies' heaving flanks and distended nostrils. Martin guiltily avoided Mrs Holland's eye as she rode up stiff with indignation.

'Thank you for trying to ruin one of my best-trained ponies,' she barked. 'As for you, Clive, I'm not surprised you can't control your pony if that's the way you've been riding her.'

Clive was dumb under this reproof, but Martin spoke up with an engaging smile.

'Oh, but, Mrs Holland, Clive said that Welsh Mountain ponies were always faster than New Forest ones, and I simply couldn't let him get away with that statement. It just wasn't fair on Bosky.'

'Well, who did win?' asked Holly with interest.

'We don't really know, 'cos the gate got in the way.'

'Alaska was pulling to the last, though, while Bosky was on a loose rein,' Clive quickly pointed out.

'Oh, but Bosky could have gone on like that for miles; he'd have worn Alaska down in the end.'

'That's enough! I'm disgusted by the whole affair. And you'll all have to keep at a walk for the next mile to cool the ponies down.'

A very subdued band trooped along through the enclosure where the pine-needles muffled the horses' hoofs. Suddenly Holly felt she must break the disapproving silence.

'Mrs Holland,' she said, 'what's the use of having a pony with a decent turn of speed if you're never allowed to have a jolly good gallop?'

'Any fool can gallop a pony. The art of riding is in collection and perfect control.'

'But if you prefer to gallop,' insisted Roy.

'Yes, why shouldn't you gallop if you want to?' piped up Miss Clegg. 'Riding's supposed to be a pleasure, isn't it, and not everybody has the same idea of pleasure.'

Mutiny was spreading through the ranks, but Mrs Holland squashed it characteristically.

'You can ruin your own horses if you like, but not mine. Other people have to ride them besides you.'

It was Rebecca who finally restored good feeling by inquiring into the breeding of the Forest ponies. In spite of her displeasure this was a subject that Mrs Holland could not resist, and she grew quite animated while the others listened with respect.

'No one quite knows how old the breed is, and it certainly got very mixed at one time. All sorts of stallions have been turned out from time to time with the idea of improving it: Queen Victoria was responsible for introducing some Arab blood, which may account for some of the fine quality you see in many of the ponies. Now there is a New Forest section of the National Pony Society stud book, and that's doing a lot towards creating a standard and type of pony that's both hardy and good looking.'

'Can anyone keep ponies in the Forest?' asked Holly.

'Certainly not. Only if they're commoners, which means people who own or rent land with common grazing rights in the Forest. Then they have to pay two and six a year for each pony, cow, or donkey they turn out.'

'Why, daddy has to pay ten shillings a week just for one field for Alaska,' said Clive.

'I suppose not many people have donkeys,' said Roy.

'Oh, yes, any number. The donkeys are almost as much natives of the Forest as the ponies.'

Talking like this they rode along a number of sandy tracks, trodden out by cattle and ponies, until a steep decline brought them down through a glade of enormous oaks. At the bottom Mrs Holland halted her pony, and pointed with her stick.

'Yonder it is, the famous Rufus Stone.'

'But it's not a stone,' said Holly, staring in disappointment at the bald metal object with some lettering on it sticking up out of ground trodden bare and scattered with rubbish left by sightseers.

'It was. But so many people wanted to carve their initials on it that metal had to be used.'

'What did you say it marked?' Rebecca asked cautiously.

'Well, it's said to be the site of the tree from which the arrow glanced that accidentally killed Rufus. But of course no one really knows; it may not have been an accident at all.'

'No one thought of looking for fingerprints on the arrow,' said Clive.

'They didn't have Scotland Yard in those days,' said Roy.

'How much more time are we going to waste looking at this old monument?' complained Miss Clegg. 'I'd much rather ride than have a history lesson.'

'It's something visitors to the Forest should see, and I like everything to be done thoroughly, including sitting on a pony at a stand,' retorted Mrs Holland. 'Sit upright, Miss Clegg, and don't loll over the pony's loins. Almost any pony but Fern would have kicked you off by now. You certainly get your money's worth of being told what to do.'

This reproof caused Miss Clegg to sulk nearly all the way home until, seeking a path of her own through the trees, she was swept clean out of the saddle by an overhanging branch. Fern, after a start of sheer surprise, stopped, and waited for her to mount again.

'There you see the advantage of a properly trained pony,' said Mrs Holland, never missing an opportunity to point a moral. 'If that had been Alaska she'd have been away at a gallop without you. By the way, I never heard exactly how it was you lost her yesterday, Clive.'

'Well – er – you see, she broke away when the stallion came up. I wasn't on her at the time.'

The other three were almost on edge as to whether Mrs Holland was going to inquire further into the meaning of the broken rein. They felt poor Clive had had quite enough ticking off for one day, but probably she imagined that not even he could be capable of anything so criminal as tying a pony up by the reins, for she only said:

'It must have given you a fright, but it turned out to be a lucky break for me.'

They all breathed again.

7

Too wild and too civilized

ALTHOUGH helping Mrs Holland with her riding school had been an amusing and interesting interlude, the four travellers were keen enough to start out next morning on a new lap of their journey. Not only did they feel the call of the unknown countryside ahead, but they were also pretty well in agreement that working for Mrs Holland would soon get very irksome.

'Mind you, she's a perfect dear, and as generous as they make them,' said Rebecca as they took the track to Lyndhurst after many farewells and exchanges of good wishes, 'but an absolute stickler for law and order. Bad as any matron.'

'All the same, a week of that would kill me,' said Roy. 'Talk about a place for everything and everything in its place! I wonder she doesn't make the ponies hang up their manes and tails on certain pegs every night.'

'I couldn't put up with all that fuss about perfect control,' added Holly. 'That Miss Clegg was a frightful idiot, but I do agree with her about galloping if you want to, even if it isn't so accomplished as doing a collected canter and changing leg on every bend. Of course, Mrs Holland's an awfully good sort—'

'Yes, she is,' said Clive. 'But when everything is so free and open like the Forest it makes you feel you want to go full out—'

'Still, you must remember that she's responsible for the children she takes out,' said Rebacca fairly. 'It wouldn't do to have them going spare all over the Forest and falling into bogs. After all, she *is* supposed to be teaching them. I can sympathize with her as I'm supposed to be in charge of you lot.'

'Oh, rot!' said Roy ungratefully, and Holly added:

'You needn't bother about us. You're only meant to be a sort of figurehead.'

'Thanks a lot!' exclaimed Rebecca, trying to sound offended, but the others only laughed, for the term of figurehead aptly described her perch on the towering Baynard.

They trotted along the winding Forest path glad to be only four instead of eight and able to choose their own pace. With their luggage strapped securely on – Clive's was now fixed to the front of the saddle – their pockets bulging with ham sandwiches cut by Miss Fry, and the glorious feeling of riding into the unknown, they were as light-hearted as the larks singing overhead in the sunny sky. It was, in fact, rather more of a venture into the unknown than they had at first realized, for there was some doubt as to whether they would be able to reach the next youth hostel that night, which would mean finding other lodgings.

There was no need for the map at first, for Mrs Holland had supplied them with full directions. They crossed the Brockenhurst road, found their way through the enclosures, and came out on the Lyndhurst road beside the Beaulieu. The river here was a gentle rippling brown stream very different from the wide gull-haunted estuary at Buckler's Hard. They met several groups of ponies with foals among them, but these were more timid than Mrs Holland's little herd, and moved away when they saw the riders.

A lively canter over a couple of miles of sandy heath brought them straight into Lyndhurst without having to pass through any ugly suburbs, It was a busy little town, the meeting place of four traffic-laden main roads, but this did not deter the Forest ponies and donkeys from pattering along the street and even suckling their foals in shop entrances, while a couple of cows ambling placidly up the main street kept a string of cars and lorries crawling behind them.

'Why, it's a real animal town,' said Clive in delight.

While the boys held the horses the girls bought some stamps and various picture postcards, mostly with Forest ponies on them.

'We'll write some at lunch time and post them in the next box we pass,' said Rebecca dutifully.

'They're horribly expensive,' complained Holly. 'Mummy and daddy will have to have one between them, and we shall have to send Cecil one 'cos he's looking after the animals, but Roy can jolly well pay for half of it.'

While they were doing this Roy had been at work with the map and compass, and announced that he had found some bridle-paths to Totton which would avoid most of the road.

'It looks like really wild country,' he promised them jubilantly.

It was certainly a lonely moor, or heath, over which he took them, without any dwelling in sight. Nor did they meet a human soul; only ponies, rough-looking cattle, hawks, and small brown birds flitting through the bushes and tufts of heather. Roy began to show some signs of uneasiness.

'What's up?' asked Holly, who was enjoying the untamed country about them, and hoping very much that they were lost.

'Funny,' he muttered. 'There are more tracks than are actually shown on the map, but none of them seems to be going in exactly the right direction.'

'Well, they all look like tracks made by animals, not foot-paths,' said Rebecca.

'Can't we just go by the compass?' asked Clive. 'So long as we keep north-east we must get home eventually.'

On the surface this seemed a very sensible suggestion, and although Roy did not much like it, coming from the youngest member, they acted upon it, choosing a path that seemed most likely to follow the compass point. It meandered downwards over the crest of the heath towards a distant valley along which ran a thin line of trees.

'I think that line of trees marks the little river we have to cross,' said Roy, a shade grudgingly.

But the horses grew more and more reluctant to go forward, and as they descended the valley the sandy surface of the track gave place to dark moist brown peat which squelched under their hoofs. Here and there it skirted pools of dark water.

Suddenly Sarah, who was in the lead, pitched violently forward, throwing Roy, map and all, over her head. She had gone in up to her knees in a bog hole.

'Gosh, we shall have to look out,' said Rebecca, as Roy picked himself up and smoothed out the crumpled map, while Sarah snuffed the hole suspiciously. 'We've been warned against bogs often enough. Perhaps we'd better turn back.'

'But if we don't get across this valley it'll be simply miles round by main road,' said Roy. 'Look, there are some cows and ponies over there. They seem to be avoiding bogs all right. Couldn't we follow them?'

'I suppose *they* should know where it's safe to go,' agreed Rebecca, and they went cautiously on.

The animals had evidently marked the riders' approach, for while they were still some way away their heads went up and they started to move off. The ground was definitely marshy, but the track winding over it seemed to have a firm bottom. For a while the ponies and cattle trotted ahead of them in the right direction, then suddenly they swung away at right angles.

'We don't want to go there, or we shall get back to Lymington,' said Roy.

'There are the tracks of more ponies and cows leading on towards the river,' said Holly. 'I'm sure it would be safe to go where they have been.'

'Our horses are heavier than unridden ponies,' objected Rebecca.

However, they went on again, although the track was getting muddied and the pools of water bigger and more frequent. At last they were faced with a stretch of slime several yards wide and with no way round. Marks showed that some cattle had recently passed through the middle of it.

'Let Crumpet go first,' said Holly. 'He's a real Forest pony, and he'll know whether it's safe or not.'

Way was made for Crumpet to take the lead. He sniffed the slime, and then without any urging crossed it in a couple of plunges. The others, not to be outdone by a small pony, came squelching in his wake. He continued to lead them unerringly through a number of equally nasty-looking places until they were close to the trees and the river. It was lonelier than ever, and there was no bridge.

'You promised us some wild country, Roy,' said Rebecca, 'but really I think I'd rather face a main road on a traffic-shy horse. It seems to me that if you were sucked down into one of these bogs no one would ever know what had happened to you. What are we going to do now?'

'The animals must have crossed, because there are tracks leading up the other bank.'

'I think it's a ford like the one we crossed the other day,' said Clive.

The river had a hard bottom of pebbles, and they were able to splash easily across. The water washed the mud off the lower parts of the horses' legs, leaving them with a curious striped appearance.

Bearing round to the left the track now took them up over a sandy heath where they met their first signs of humanity, a gipsy encampment by a patch of fir-trees. This high ridge marked the Forest boundary, for on the northward side there was suddenly unfolded before them a panorama of pastures and fields of young crops with farms scattered among them. This view made a striking contrast with the wild country through which they had just come, and which rolled away behind them to the dusky bank of Forest trees on the far horizon. Holly felt a pang of sadness as she looked upon the cultivated land to the north. As if voicing her thoughts Roy said:

'Well, it's almost good-bye to the Forest. This path should bring us down to a road where those houses are.'

'What do we do then?' asked Clive.

'Eling is our next landmark. There's a drive to it through a sort of park which cuts off a lot of road.'

'Well, a park sounds safe enough,' said Rebecca. 'But first what about lunch? It's nearly two o'clock.'

They decided to eat it at once while they were still on the edge of the Forest. Although there was a nice stretch of grass where the horses could graze, there were no trees or fence to tie them too. This meant holding the ropes all the time, which made a difficult business both of eating and of writing post-cards.

'I suppose I ought to send a card to Joshua as he's looking after Kelly,' said Holly. 'Which do you think he'd like best, some Forest ponies or a view of the Rufus Stone?'

'Neither,' said Roy. 'He wouldn't see any point in the stone, and he'd hate to think of ponies roaming free.'

Acting on Mr Granger's instructions they gave the horses an hour's rest, although this brought it well on into the after-noon before they saddled up again and rode out of the Forest.

'Poor little Crumpet, you may never see it again,' said Holly.

Crumpet did look rather despondent, but he had come a long way through tiring going without being as fit as the others. She felt her depression over his smallness creeping back. She had been elated by Mrs Holland's praise of him and his intelligence over gates and bogs, but if he were going to flag half-way through each day all the enjoyment of exploring would be spoilt. The fact of not knowing how far they had yet to ride before finding somewhere to stay was no longer so attractive as in the morning.

'This must be the gate into the park,' said Roy, breaking in upon her gloomy thoughts. 'A pity about the notice saying "Private".'

They agreed it was a great pity when he showed them on the map how the path through the park cut off a big loop of road. A girl riding by on a chestnut pony looked at them with the interest one rider always feels for others.

'I say,' Rebecca called out, 'do you know if we can get through here?'

'Well you *can*, but the keeper who lives in the middle chases you if he sees you, and he has a gun. As you're strangers I should risk it.'

'We can ride faster than he could run,' said Holly.

'He could shoot faster than we could gallop,' demurred Clive.

'I don't think he'd actually shoot,' said the girl. 'It would be against the law to kill you even if you were trespassing.'

So they resolved to brave the armed keeper, and the girl wished them good luck as they rode into the park. An un-surfaced drive ran straight between tall spindly trees. They trotted warily along, keeping to the softest parts to muffle the horses' hoofs. The 'kookerook!' of pheasants in the under-growth startled them, and kept the picture of the keeper's gun before their eyes. At last the outlines of some buildings showed through the trees.

'This'll be where the keeper lives,' whispered Roy. 'I vote we ride up as quietly as possible to the edge of the trees and then gallop for it.'

So when they came to the last trees they applied their legs sharply to their horses' sides, and swept like a cavalry charge across the open space in front of the small farm, Alaska buck-ing perilously. No dogs flew out. No angry voice hailed them. Only a cow in a paddock stared after them in astonishment as they gained the shelter of the woods beyond. Evidently the keeper was not at home, but the panic once started held them well in its grip, and they galloped helter-skelter on under the dusky trees for a full mile until a gate appeared at the end of the drive. This led them on to a public lane under a notice which stated not only 'Private' but 'No thoroughfare'.

Once out of danger they rode more slowly along the wind-ing lane between fields. Seeing some cattle gathered round a stone trough in a field Holly said:

'I wonder if the horses are thirsty?'

'Let's try them.'

They opened the gate and the horses made a rush for the trough, scattering the cattle and sucking up the water like so many pumps.

'I say, we shall have to remember this,' said Roy. 'The poor old things must have been thirsty for ages.'

The horses perked up after their drink, but they had not continued many steps down the lane when a shout was heard and a stout man hurried after them.

'Next time you want to give your beasts a drink how about asking permission first?'

The three younger ones were abashed by his obvious annoyance, but Rebecca replied coldly:

'In the first place we didn't see anyone to ask, and also it never occurred to us that anyone could mind us giving a thirsty horse a drink. I'm sorry we did not see you.'

'People here don't seem nearly so friendly as the ones in the New Forest,' Clive remarked.

'It must be the difference between living where the country is open and free and where it's divided up and everybody watches jealously over their little bit,' said Rebecca.

Although Eling had looked like a village on the map they soon found that it had been swallowed up in a tide of red houses, factories, stores, and mills stretching right from Totton. It was a dreary area, and the horses filed in a depressed manner along the gutters of the busy streets. Baynard, with his ears back and his tail clamped down, kept a nervous eye on the traffic.

'How much of this have we got to go through?' asked Rebecca.

'About a mile and a half, till we get over the Test,' replied Roy apologetically, as if the encroachments of the town were his fault.

As they were half-way across a great concrete railway bridge an express train screamed and rattled underneath. All the horses flung up their heads in alarm, and Baynard bounded forward, shied away from a pantechnicon looming through the smoke left by the express, slipped badly, and came down on his side in the road. Rebecca came off in the gutter, but had the presence of mind to keep hold of the rein.

Roy promptly jumped off Sarah, and seeing that Rebecca was all right, tried to examine Baynard's knees from which blood was oozing. But the frightened horse would not stand still, and the traffic was grinding and hooting round them. A double-decker bus had halted sharply behind them as Baynard fell, and a man who had jumped off it cried:

'Get them off the bridge before another train comes.'

He took the offside rein and helped Rebecca to lead Baynard, whose great size and strength now became alarmingly apparent. The others, who had also jumped off, followed leading their mounts. Under the stranger's guidance they crossed a second bridge, this time over the Test, and turned up a quiet by-road through allotments.

'Now we can have a look at the damage,' he said, putting down a portfolio he had been carrying under one arm.

Rebecca, who had quickly pulled herself together after her shaking, got out the first-aid box and treated Baynard's cuts with professional skill.

'Thank heavens they're not deep! No need for stitches, but he must be a bit bruised, poor old fellow.'

'There's a cut on his stifle, but it's not bad,' said the man. 'You've both had a lucky escape. That road is poisonous for horses; you must be strangers round here to have tried it. Where are you bound?'

'To Romney Marsh,' said Holly.

'But – but that's away in Kent!'

He stared in astonishment at the four riders and at the horses who, their fright quickly forgotten, were tearing at the dusty roadside grass. Then, noticing the bundles attached to their saddles and Roy's rucksack: 'Oh, I get it now, you're on a riding tour. Come from the New Forest?'

'Yes, and we live in Kent,' explained Clive.

The man who, although he was quite young, wore a short dark beard, seemed struck with his new and very chance acquaintances.

'You know, that's just what I'd like to do if only I had the time. But I'd avoid anything like the Southampton district! You ought to head for where I live – some of the best riding country in the south of England.'

'Where's that?' asked Holly.

'Goodwood.'

'But that's a racecourse,' said Roy.

'Quite right. But that's not all there is to it by a long chalk.

I say, I wish you would try it. If you're going to Romney Marsh it's pretty well on your way. I've got an old horse at home, an ex-chaser, very ex, I'm afraid. If you cared to give me a ring when you're near I could show you some marvellous bridle-paths through the woods and over the downs. There's a Roman road you could ride along.'

'Oh, it does sound heavenly, a racecourse and downs and a Roman road!' cried Holly. 'Do let's go! Is it far, Roy?'

'We couldn't get there today, I'm sure,' said Roy.

'No, it would be a couple of days from here,' agreed the bearded young man. 'I tell you what, I'm sure we could put you up for the night. Here's my card with the phone number. Give me a ring the night before. I must fly now and get another bus.'

He thrust a card into Holly's hand, picked up his portfolio, and before anyone thought of thanking him for his help was running back along the road.

'Well, I'm jiggered!' exclaimed Roy, voicing the surprise of them all. 'He's a quick-moving bloke!'

'It was jolly decent of him to get off his bus to help us,' said Rebecca. 'Now I'm afraid he'll have to buy another ticket.'

'We will go to Goodwood, won't we?' asked Holly.

'And stay with a complete stranger? Oh, I don't think we ought to do that.'

'But we stay with strangers at other places,' said Clive.

'That's different where you pay, silly.'

'Seems to me a good wheeze to have one night where we don't pay,' remarked Roy.

'I think *you're* silly, Rebecca,' added Holly. 'How could any-thing happen to four of us? He couldn't lock us in a cellar and hold us for ransom.'

'Well, what we've got to decide now is where to put up *to-night*.' Rebecca shelved the subject. 'Any chance of reaching a youth hostel?'

'Not a hope,' said Roy. 'Finding our way through those bogs, and then this awful road, has taken us twice as long as I thought it would.'

'Crumpet's tired, Baynard's shaken up, and so am I, for that matter, so let's start looking for an inn at once.'

Inns that had room for four travellers seemed few and far between. They tried at Rowham without success, and then, hitting upon the Chilworth Drove, found themselves going deep into woods. They trotted for a mile through trees and bracken without seeing a soul, let alone a house, while the shadows lengthened and the light grew dim.

'Are you sure we're not going in circles, Roy?'

'Not by the compass. We ought to be out of the woods and into Chilworth at any minute.'

'My back's aching terribly. Can't we stop soon?' complained Clive.

'What's the use of stopping in the middle of a wood,' snapped Holly.

At last they did come out into the village, only to find that there was still nowhere to stay.

'You might be able to get in at Romsey,' said the innkeeper, who could not take them himself.

But Romsey meant turning almost on their tracks, and Roy, looking at the map, said it was a town with another main road. The horses, hungry as well as tired, were tearing eagerly at the wayside grass.

'We shall have to sleep out and arrange pickets to stay up and mind the horses,' said Holly.

'What about feeding ourselves?' said Roy faintly. 'Let's try the next village, Chandler's Ford.'

'It sounds nice and countrified; a village by a ford,' said Rebecca.

They started off with renewed hope along a bridle-path, only to come out after a few fields upon another slippery main road.

'This is no better than Totton,' groaned Rebecca as Baynard, his nerves still shaken, sidled along in the gutter trembling at the double-decker buses.

'I don't see a hope of getting anywhere for the horses,' said Holly. 'Whatever shall we do?'

'There's a kind of hotel just ahead,' said Clive.

The hotel Clive had spotted had several big sleek cars drawn up outside, and it did not look the kind of place likely to welcome four tousled riders and their tired horses.

'I know, you go and ask, Clive,' said Rebecca. 'They might take pity on you, being the youngest.'

Clive plucked up enough courage to go and ring the bell. No one answered, although several people were strolling in and out, so in answer to repeated signals from the others he went inside. He reappeared after several minutes, followed by a majestic yellow-haired lady in a black gown.

'So you really have got horses!' she exclaimed. 'I thought the little chap was having me on. Well, my little girl will be just thrilled.'

'We can have two double rooms,' said Clive proudly. 'And this lady say that the horses can have the tennis court.'

'The tennis court!' exclaimed the others.

'It won't do it much good,' added Roy.

'Oh, no one plays tennis there, it's like a hayfield,' said the hotel lady. 'My hubby will be only too glad to have it eaten down a bit. I'll get him to show you the way in.'

She fetched her small grey husband, who seemed delighted with the unusual guests. After locking saddles and bridles in one of the garages he led them through a garden gate and along a narrow path full of sharp turns between rose-trees and flower borders. It was a little difficult to get Baynard round some of the corners, and Alaska shied at some washing and narrowly missed putting her foot through a garden frame. Eventually they arrived safely on the tennis court behind the hotel, which bore a thick crop of clover and rye grass. Down went the horses heads the moment they got inside the wire netting, and all signs of weariness vanished as they attacked the feast.

'I'll tell the gardener to fetch a tub and fill it with water for them,' said the hotel proprietor.

After making sure the wire was safe all the way round, and winding up the ragged remains of the net which still sagged across the court, the riders were shown to their rooms. These had the advantage of looking out towards the tennis court, so that they had the horses right under their eyes.

'I can hardly believe that both the horses and us are all comfortably settled for the night when only half an hour ago everything looked so hopeless,' said Holly. 'And of all unlikely places too!'

'It just shows you should never give up hope,' said Rebecca. 'Look, there's the old gardener taking out their water, and the little girl giving them carrots through the wire must be the one belonging to the hotel, They really are in clover tonight! I say, what about hot baths!'

8

Lost on the Hampshire Downs

It was pleasant next morning not to have any chores or stable-work to do other than grooming, and they were able to start in good time without having to get up early. Rebecca inspected Baynard's knees anxiously, and was relieved that the small grazes were already beginning to heal. Roy, who had been studying his beloved maps at breakfast, said there was a youth hostel at Soberton, only sixteen miles away, so for Baynard's sake they were glad not to have to hurry.

Having to go through nearly five miles of an industrial area, which had grown up round Chandler's Ford and Eastleigh, also slowed them down, and they were thankful to cross the Itchen and get into the rich agricultural country beyond. They bought the ingredients for a picnic lunch at a village shop, and ate it where the horses could enjoy a strip of clover beside a lonely lane. Avoiding Bishop's Waltham, which they feared might be another built-up area, Roy successfully brought them by narrow lanes and bridle-paths to the tiny village of Upham, where the kind landlord of the Brushmakers' Arms gave the thirsty horses a drink of water.

By the time they reached a long valley, ominously called The Hungers, they noticed that the cultivated countryside was slowly but unmistakably changing to lofty downland. One of Roy's bridle-paths unfortunately ended in a low but solid stile, and Holly wondered anxiously whether Crumpet would be able to jump it.

'I'll give you a lead,' said Rebecca, for to Baynard it was only a step.

When Crumpet's turn came he skipped over it as neatly as

a rabbit, and raised himself several points in Holly's esteem.

The youth hostel stood high on a ridge just beyond Soberton, and they were not long in finding a farm where the farmer at once said the horses could spend the night in his stackyard, which was knee-deep in good grass.

Once in the hostel the warden was not long in setting them to work on peeling a tubful of potatoes, and while they were doing this Roy said:

'We're only a day's ride from Goodwood. What about ringing up that man?'

Holly fished the crumpled card from her pocket.

'Noel Welbeck – Commercial Artist,' she read out. 'His telephone number is Singleton.'

'There's no hostel on the downs between here and Arundel. If we don't stay with him it'll mean finding another inn.'

'Oh, very well,' said Rebecca, who had demurred at first.

Holly got through after supper. Mr Welbeck was out, and his father answered the telephone. He sounded rather cross, but after a slight misunderstanding he said he supposed it would be all right for them to come 'if Noel arranged it'.

'Well, if he lives with his father that makes it more respectable,' said Rebecca, drowning the last of her doubts between the verses of a song which the hostellers were loudly singing in the common-room.

At breakfast next morning Roy made the exciting discovery from a youth, who had arrived late the previous night, that they were only a few miles from Hambledon, the home of English cricket and the famous Hambledon Club.

'Just think, the place where Silver Billy played! The chap they called the Father of English Cricket. We must go there in case we never get such a chance again.'

'Is it good riding country?' asked Holly.

'It's right in the middle of the downs,' said the youth. 'I came by road, but there were lots of tracks that 'ud be all right for horses.'

'Yes, we simply must go,' agreed Clive, who, although he

did not know much cricket history, felt Roy should be supported
in this honourably masculine form of hero-worship.

'Well, one place is as good as another to me, so long as there
are no bogs or industrial areas,' said Rebecca.

They were not long in coming to Hambledon by tracks con-
necting scattered farms set among huge fields of young corn,
and Clive and Roy had the satisfaction of riding over Windmill Down, where Silver Billy had once driven his now legen-
dary balls.

'But there's Broad Halfpenny Down too,' said Roy, 'another
place where the club played. This bridle-path on the map
should take us round the side of it.'

They were now well out on the Hampshire downs, which un-
dulated for as far as they could see, partly wooded and riddled
with enticing white tracks. Although they rode for nearly an
hour they saw only flocks of black-faced Hampshire Down
sheep with glossy rooks feeding among them, occasionally a
startled hare, and larks singing high above.

'When is this Broad Halfpenny Down coming up?'
Rebecca inquired at last.

Roy had been puckering his forehead over the map for some
time. At a spot where four tracks met the others stopped and
looked inquiringly at him. He dismounted, and, placing Mr
Fowle's compass on a gate-post, studied it carefully.

'I'm flummoxed,' he confessed at last. 'We seem to have come
down the track we ought to be going up.'

Clive and Holly dismounted too; they turned the map this
way and that, compared the lines of latitude with the compass,
and looked unavailingly for landmarks. Then they began to
argue about the various right- and left-hand turns they had
taken without coming to any helpful conclusion, except that
they must have passed Broad Halfpenny Down without knowing it.

'Then where are we aiming now?' asked Rebecca, who had
remained mounted. 'I don't mean Goodwood, but the next place
name on the map.'

'Clanfield, and then Charlton,' said Roy. 'That would put us on a line of bridle-paths to Singleton, which is close to Good-wood.'

'Oh, yes, the Welbecks' address is Singleton,' said Holly.

Rebecca stood up in her stirrups to command a better view, and said:

'I can see a chimney along that valley. There might be some-body we could ask.'

The chimney belonged to a cottage, so deserted-looking that they thought it was empty until they heard the muffled strains of a wireless. Roy tapped on the door. It opened a few inches and a woman's dark face peered furtively out. She regarded him in silence while he asked if she could tell them the best path to take to Clanfield, and at last replied in a thick, guttural voice:

'I not know all der way. Go there,' pointing to the left, 'an' you find der bull, dey vill tell you.'

She shut the door immediately.

'Just our luck that the only human for miles round should be a foreigner!'

'What on earth did she mean by "der bull"?' said Rebecca.

'She said "they" would tell us, so it's more than one,' said Roy.

'P'r'aps it's a pub,' said Holly, but the others scorned this idea.

'No trade for a pub out here!'

They decided to take the path pointed out by the woman, and cantered along its smooth turf for nearly two miles until Baynard's luggage began to work loose, and Rebecca had to stop and tighten the straps.

'How does your rucksack work?' she asked Roy.

'Things get in a bit of a jumble by the end of the day.'

Another half-hour passed. Holly next pointed out some cattle feeding below them in the valley, and suggested going to see if one was a bull. Then over the next brow some build-ings appeared. They trotted on, although the way was steep and the horses rather slack, and Clive, who was in the lead, called:

'Holly's right, it is a pub! Guess what's it's called!'

They had come out at cross-roads on one corner of which stood an inn called the Bat and Ball, with a man's portrait for its sign.

'That woman meant "Ball", not "Bull".'

'And, do you know, I believe that's a picture of Silver Billy himself,' said Roy reverently.

With the help of the inn and the cross-roads Roy was easily able to find where they were on the map, not far from Clanfield. When they reached the village they bought a loaf and some biscuits and cheese, but as they climbed the grassy flank of Windmill Hill, topped by the stark ruin of an ancient mill, a clap of thunder startled them, and they suddenly became aware of black clouds rolling up over Charlton Down.

'Looks as if we're for it!' said Rebecca. 'Better find some shelter quickly.'

'Let's eat our grub first before it gets wet,' suggested Holly.

They were only half-way through the meal when the storm broke. Lightning flickered over the bald crest of the down, now grey against the blue-black sky, and the rain leaped down upon them with a roar like that of an approaching train.

At first the horses veered about on their ropes in a vain attempt to avoid the fury, then, resigning themselves to the elements, stood with backs humped to the wind and drooping heads, flinching at each clap of thunder. The water sleeked their coats and coursed in rivulets down their flanks and limbs. The riders cowered under some bushes, trying to make themselves as small as possible, Clive had struggled into his mackintosh, but the other three soon began to feel the rain soaking through to their skins. They finished their food, though the water poured off their noses and turned the biscuits to pap as they bit into them.

The rain ceased as suddenly as it began. A beam of sunlight slanted down the valley and lit a million glittering points of light among the leaves and grasses. With chattering teeth and numbed fingers they bridled the cantankerous horses. Sarah snapped at Alaska, and Alaska kicked out at Crumpet, who squealed like a pig. Then Baynard in turning stepped on Roy's foot and there was another outcry. They dragged themselves on to sodden saddles, and the reins felt like bits of water-weed between their fingers. The sun grew stronger as the storm clouds retreated over the downs and bathed in mocking beams the bedraggled crew plodding down the gleaming road.

'It's a good thing we've somewhere fixed to stay tonight,' said Rebecca.

'If they don't turn us away when they see what awful wrecks we look,' said Holly gloomily, remembering the cross voice on the telephone.

Once through Charlton they struck a bridle-path running straight and true towards the Sussex border.

'Let's have a warm up,' suggested Clive, giving Alaska her head.

They felt better after a gallop to the top of the slope. Clouds of steam rose from the horses, and their warmth combined with the wind began to dry their riders' clothes.

'Listen, you chaps,' said Roy importantly. 'We've crossed the county boundary into Sussex.'

They looked about them with due regard, but there did not seem to be a great deal of difference between the country in front and behind.

'Sussex makes Kent sound awfully near,' sighed Holly.

'Sussex is a long, long county,' Roy reassured her.

Later they came to the conclusion that Sussex was steeper than Hampshire. The horses laboured up the hills, and where the rain had made the tracks greasy slid down them, so that their pace was slowed for a time. At Compton, deep in a hollow, the air was languid and heavy with the scent of rain-washed flowers and leaves, but up on the other side of the valley it was keen enough to make them shiver.

Finding Crumpet beginning to flag Holly trudged up and down the steepest hills on foot, and when Roy said they were within a few miles of Singleton she asked if they couldn't stop for a bit and let the horses rest.

'They could do with some grass too,' she added. 'The rain made them much too miserable to graze.'

'It might be a good chance to have a bit of a tidy up too,' said Rebecca. 'We certainly do look frights.'

So while the horses were feeding they took off their coats and spread them on a nearby fence in the sun and wind. This gave their damp shirts a chance to dry too. Rebecca got a comb and mirror out of her luggage, and they squatted round trying to make themselves look more presentable. The comb dragged painfully through their wet, tousled hair, in which bits of twig and leaves were entangled. Rebecca tried to make further improvements with the use of powder and lipstick.

'You can have some powder, Holly. It'll cover up your dirty face.'

Holly thought this a good idea, but she used the powder so freely that she made herself look like a clown, and in wiping off the excess with a grubby handkerchief left behind a number of dark smears. The boys, who had contented themselves with tugging the comb through their hair, laughed scornfully at these beauty aids.

'It wouldn't matter if we were only staying at a hostel,' said Rebecca.

'The old man didn't sound as if we'd be very welcome,' said Holly. 'Probably his son Noel is like Roy, always inviting people on the spur of the moment.'

'Does Roy do that?' asked Clive quickly, and she realized that she had been the reverse of tactful.

Roy raised his eyebrows, but their embarrassment was cut short by a cry from Rebecca. Baynard had trodden on her sponge bag, which she had left on the ground, and burst a tube of toothpaste over the rest of the contents.

They packed up again and rode down through hanging woods into the mellow old village of West Dean. From there the road to Singleton was short and direct.

'We'd better begin asking where this man lives in case we overshoot it,' said Rebecca.

The only person in sight just then was a boy of about nine straddling the parapet of a little bridge. He had been watching their approach, and as they drew nearer beckoned to them mysteriously.

'Are you the four horsemen of the Apocalypse?'

They looked from one to another blankly.

'Are we?'

'There are four of us,' pointed out Clive.

'I guess you're the ones he meant,' the boy nodded.

'Do you mean Mr Welbeck?' asked Rebecca.

'That's him. I'm waiting to show you where he lives.'

The house to which he led them was hidden, all but the thatched roof, behind a high wall of smooth flints set in cement. A lime-tree drooped its scented boughs over the wall along with those of purple and white lilacs.

'I'll go and fetch him out to you,' said the boy, opening a blue garden door.

But at that moment there was the sound of rapid steps and out came the artist himself.

'I heard your hoof-beats coming through the village,' he greeted them. 'Welcome to Goodwood!'

T—FRH—D

9

A night near Goodwood

THE shyness that the riders had felt over presenting themselves like this to a strange household was quickly thawed by the warmth of Noel Welbeck's greeting. He lost no time in getting to know their names, and those of the horses, and inquired after Baynard's injuries.

'His cuts are healing up fine; it was a jolly lucky escape,' said Rebecca. 'I hope you got another bus.'

'Oh, I managed,' said the artist cheerily. 'What I hope is that you'll approve of the arrangements I've made for your horses. The farm where I keep my old fellow couldn't take any more because they've overstocked, but they let me have some fodder and I've got the use of some stabling in the village for the night. Come on, Gordon, you can help settle them in.'

Accompanied by the little boy he showed them the way to a yard surrounded by rows of loose boxes.

'My word, what a lot of boxes!' exclaimed Roy.

'And not a single horse among the lot,' added Clive.

'They're mostly only in use when the races are on,' explained Noel. 'It's a very different sight during race week, with horses coming and going and grooms and lads scurrying about the place.'

They chose four boxes in a row, and Noel and the little boy brought some straw from a shed and spread it on the floors. The yard bore a thick crop of purple clover and rye grass, and at first the horses were far more keen to get at this than to go into the magnificent loose-boxes. But when a bag of oats and chaff was produced they changed their minds and went straight to the mangers.

'There won't be any rolling in the mud tonight, so they'll be nice and quick to groom tomorrow,' said Rebecca. 'Baynard looks rather handsome in these surroundings.'

'Poor old Crumpet can hardly see over the door,' said Holly.

'Couldn't get any hay, I'm afraid,' said Noel. 'But I brought along father's swap because I thought if we cut them each a good pile of this clover grass they'd enjoy it more than dry stuff.'

While they took it in turns to cut and collect up the green food, Gordon lugged buckets of water from a nearby tap. He was a solemn little fellow of few words, and insisted on examining the horses, feeling their legs and looking at their teeth in the manner of a hardened old dealer.

'He's mad on horses and just lives for race week,' said Noel. 'He comes from the farm, and he's really very useful because he gets my old horse ready when I want to ride. He has to stand on the manger to get the bridle on, of course. His name is really John, but he insists on being called Gordon after Gordon Richards.'

Gordon came out of Baynard's box looking serious.

'You know, that chestnut was favouring his off fore coming through the village. There's no heat now, but I guess you'll see some swelling after he's stood in all night.'

'I didn't notice anything wrong,' said Rebecca with alarm.

They all felt Baynard's leg in turn without finding anything amiss.

'I think you must have imagined the limping, Gordon,' said Noel.

'I didn't say "limping", I said he was *favouring* it.'

'Perhaps he knocked it and went short for a few paces,' Roy suggested.

They agreed that this might be the solution, though really they believed that Gordon was making it up.

'Better come and see my parents now,' said Noel.

'We're rather a lot to come at such short notice,' Rebecca began to apologize, but he cut her short with:

'Oh, they're used to people turning up at any old time.'

Inside the blue door drifts of flowers poured their scent out on the evening air. A bent old man in baggy trousers and a much-darned coat was vigorously mowing the lawn. They thought he was a jobbing gardener until Noel said, 'This is my father,' and introduced them one at a time.

Mr Welbeck senior peered at them with sharp little eyes set under an overhanging brow.

'And so you're Polly,' he said, boring into Holly.

'Holly, father!'

'She was Polly on the phone. Why do they call you Holly now? Have you grown prickles?'

Before Holly could find a reply his eyes darted on to Rebecca.

'And you, what do you do?'

'I'm a nurse.'

'A nurse, eh? What a waste: there's nobody ill here! Must think up a new complaint I haven't had before. Boys? You don't have to tell me what *you* do. I know all about boys. Take them to your mother, Noel, she may know where to put them.'

At this moment Mrs Welbeck herself appeared from the house wearing slacks and a jacket embroidered with Chinese dragons. She greeted them each with an affectionate embrace, exclaiming:

'Oh, I'm so glad you've come. Don't tell me your names because I shan't remember them, but I do know you're the ones with the horses. Where are the dear darlings?'

'We left them in the stables, mother. I didn't think there'd be room for them here.'

'Quite right, Noel, how sensible you are! The girls can have the spare room – there are two beds there – and didn't you say something about the studio for the boys?'

'That was the idea, if they don't mind the smell of turps.'

'I like it,' Roy assured him.

Although the Welbecks were quite unlike any family they knew at home, the visitors quickly became at ease with them. They soon got accustomed to Mr Welbeck's sudden remarks and Mrs Welbeck's vague kindliness, while Noel's good nature seemed boundless. At supper they were pressed to tell some of their adventures, to the entertainment of father and son and the astonishment of the mother, who kept leaving the room to fetch forgotten dishes and returning in time to hear some point which she connected with what she had heard before going out.

'My son has a horse, you know,' said Mr Welbeck. 'Only got three legs, but it seems to hop around all right.'

'I'll show you the way over the Trundle tomorrow,' said Noel.

'What's the Trundle?' asked Clive.

'It's that terrific hill you can see from the garden, and which overlooks the racecourse. It's an old earthwork of some kind. Once up there you can see for miles, and I can put you on some bridle-paths that will take you right into Arundel. That's where you're aiming?'

'Yes, there's a youth hostel there.'

'Thought you were staying at the castle with the duke,' said Mr Welbeck.

By the time they had explored the village and cleaned their saddles and bridles in honour of Goodwood it was dark and time to turn in. Rebecca and Holly shared a little blue room with check curtains and patchwork bedspreads. There was a scent of pot-pourri and beeswax, and they undressed by the light of candles set in china fishes standing upright on their painted tails. The house was lit entirely by lamps and candles because of Mr Welbeck's hatred of anything electric. Clive and Roy had been lighted across the garden to the studio by a hurricane lantern, and settled down giggling in company with a human skeleton and a stuffed stag which Noel had been using as models.

'One of the things I like about this ride is not knowing what kind of people you're going to meet each night,' said Rebecca, as they got into bed. 'Look at the Welbecks, how different they are from Miss Fry and Mrs Holland, and how different they were from the hotel people and the Fowles too.'

'And yet they're all nice in their own way,' said Holly. 'It must be the horses that make people like us. I expect that farmer at Soberton wouldn't have been half so helpful if we had come in a motor caravan.'

Sleep, as usual, came rapidly, and morning seemed upon them almost before they had dented their pillows. Joining the boys, who had not slept quite so soundly on the studio floor, they hurried off to feed the horses before breakfast.

'How did you get on with the skeleton?' asked Holly.

'He was a quiet old chap, never said a word all night,' replied Roy. 'But Clive did nothing but snore.'

'I didn't!' exclaimed Clive indignantly. 'It was an owl.'

'A human owl,' Roy was retorting as they turned in at the yard, but the words died on his lips. The door of Sarah's box was standing wide open.

'Sarah's got out!' cried Holly at the same second.

'You couldn't have shot the bolt properly last night,' said Rebecca.

'Oh, but I did! I know I did. Somebody must have let her out.'

Roy dashed back to the road, and looked up and down its empty length.

'It's funny that she should leave the others, and all this clover too,' said Holly.

Clive, struck by a sudden thought, ran to look in the box where they had left their saddlery.

'Roy, her saddle and bridle are gone too!'

'Then she's been stolen! I'm going to the police straight away.'

'Wait a mo,' said Rebecca, catching his arm. 'I really can't believe a thief would pick on one so easily recognized as a skew-bald. And another thing, how would a stranger know the right saddle and bridle to use?'

While Roy was hesitating Holly, who had been scanning the surrounding country, cried:

'Look, up on that hill by the trees!'

They looked up at the hill rising above the roofs of the vil-lage, and there, cantering across the side, went a skewbald horse with a very small rider in the saddle. Almost at once they vanished behind the trees.

'It's that boy they call Gordon!' exclaimed Roy, becoming quite pale with rage. 'How dare he take Sarah out without asking? If he brings her back lame or hurt in any way I'll – I'll kill him!'

He wanted to get out one of the other horses and go in pursuit, but the others managed to persuade him against this.

'Gordon's far more likely to get in a panic and let Sarah trip galloping downhill if he sees you charging after him,' said Rebecca. 'If they come back at their own pace there'll be no harm done.'

'No harm done!' muttered Roy, pacing round the yard, while the others got busy feeding and grooming their own mounts.

'If Gordon doesn't bring Sarah back without a scratch there really will be a murder,' remarked Holly. 'I haven't seen him so mad for ages.'

The echo of hoofs through the village announced when Gordon was on his way home. He came riding jauntily into the yard, Sarah eager for her breakfast, but when he saw the others his face was a study in dismay.

'Ooh, I didn't bank on you being so early!'

He dismounted as if the saddle were red hot.

'No, I don't suppose you did!' said Roy between his teeth, gripping the rein. 'Who said you could take my mare out?'

'I didn't ask in case you said no,' replied Gordon candidly. While Roy was digesting the logic of this he went on : 'My, she's a first-rate ride, and I'm not a bit sorry really that I took her. So you can knock me down if you want to.'

Faced with the culprit Roy found himself unable to knock down a boy at least five years younger than himself. Seeing that Sarah was none the worse for her outing, and mollified by Gordon's praise of her, his anger began to subside.

'I could wipe the floor with you, and you deserve it,' he said. 'But I suppose there wouldn't be much point now, as you'll never have a chance to pinch Sarah again.'

'Of course not,' agreed Gordon. 'And if you like to go and have breakfast I'll muck out and groom her for you.'

As the others had finished their stable work Roy consented to this offer of atonement. Just as they were leaving Clive said sharply to Gordon:

'Don't go trying any more horses. The grey is very hot indeed, and needs a terrifically good rider to manage her. If she gets you off she'll savage you with her teeth and hoofs. She's killed three people already.'

The other three were more amazed by this revelation of Alaska's character than Gordon, who replied loftily:

'Haven't time to ride any more, even if you asked me to. I've got to get Mr Welbeck's horse ready after this. He's a real chaser, won races and in the book too!'

After breakfast they took the horses round to the house because Mr and Mrs Welbeck were anxious to see them. Mrs Welbeck lavished praise and sugar lumps on them all.

Mr Welbeck gave each horse in turn more critical attention.

'Great diversity of types,' he remarked at length. 'Good thing that. I detest uniformity.'

After saying good-bye they went with Noel to the farm where he kept his horse, Harkover. Gordon had certainly been very busy, for he had put a good polish on Sarah's coat, and now he appeared from the farm stables leading Harkover, a grand bay horse nearly as tall as Baynard, and rather better proportioned. Noel looked to his girths and then swung himself into the saddle and they started out on the next lap of their journey, leaving Gordon gazing wistfully after them.

Harkover cantered along joyfully, his good looks only marred by the thickened tendons of one foreleg. His presence put new life into the other four, who had become a little sobered by constant journeying. They all tossed their heads and capered a little.

A white hard lane led up the hill out of the village, beside a thick belt of trees fringing the park. Although it was only ten in the morning the sun was hot enough to make the horses sweat, particularly Alaska, who was determined to keep pace with the two bigger horses. The long hill soon began to tell on Crumpet's short steps, and although Holly dismounted up the steepest stretch he fell behind. She was mortified by the others having to stop and wait for her.

'We'll have to give you a tow,' said Noel.

But to Holly it was no joke.

'I do hope he'll be able to get home before he's quite worn out,' she said.

At intervals big white boards announced the way to the differently priced car parks, and the nearer to the course the more expensive these became. Near the top of the great hill the roof of the grandstand came into view against the trees, and at last they were riding beside the racecourse itself. They stopped to rest the horses and to admire the breath-taking way in which the green band of level turf swept in a great arc high up round the hillside as if terraced out by giant hands. Below it the hill dropped away down to Singleton and Charlton, and the country spread out in smiling early summer leafage to the Surrey and Hampshire borders.

Goodwood was completely deserted. The car park notice boards spoke to a motorless countryside; only the horses' hoof-beats broke the stillness of the hillside and the deep woods looming behind the racecourse.

'Of course this all looks very different during race week,' said Noel. 'The cars crawl bumper to bumper, and unless you've got a grand-stand seat you're lucky if you see more than the jockeys' silk shirts and a glimpse of horses' manes.'

'I should come up here every day if I lived at Singleton,' said Holly.

'I do mostly. I try to make sketches of the race-goers.'

They rode past the grand-stand, which from the back resembled a great theatre or stadium, while round it stood a little town of solid buildings – betting and totalizator stands, clubs, restaurants, changing rooms, and quarters for jockeys, trainers, and attendants. Goodwood seemed like a deserted town from which the inhabitants had only lately gone, leaving everything clean and smartly painted.

'I hope the horses are impressed by their surroundings,' said Rebecca, breaking the spell.

'They ought to be,' said Roy. 'It's the nearest to a racecourse these four will ever get.'

'Has Harkover raced here?' asked Clive.

'Oh, no, he's not a flat-racer,' replied Harkover's owner a shade indignantly. 'But he's jumped the course at Aintree more than once. Too bad your day is done, old boy.'

He stroked Harkover's neck, and the old horse tossed his head as if reliving some former triumph.

'Well, now, it's time we got on to the bridle-paths. I can't come with you all the way as I have some work to finish, but I'll put you right for Arundel.'

He led them under the trees beyond the grand-stand. Although all was green overhead the horses' legs rustled deeply through drifts of dead leaves accumulated from many autumns. The paths got more and more like tunnels scooped by moles through a green soil until at last they came out into a lane. A very short way down here Noel showed them a gate leading on to another woodland path.

' 'Fraid I must leave you here,' he said. 'This gate opens on to the Roman road of Stane Street which leads straight to Bignor Hill. But before you get to the top of the hill you'll meet a kind of cross track. Turn sharply down to the right, and make for Madehurst. You should find your way easily enough from there to Arundel.'

When they thanked him for all his help he smiled through his beard and said:

'We've all enjoyed it, and you've cheered father up a lot. He gets a bit depressed about the modern world, and it's done him good to meet some people who prefer travelling across country on horseback to scorching along the road on machines. Well, cheerio, and if you meet with any Romans give them my kind regards!'

He turned back towards Goodwood, Harkover's tail streaming out jauntily as he strode up the hill, and the others passed through the wooden gate on to Stane Street.

10

Enter Ebony

ON the Roman road at last, Holly's romantic mind immediately began to picture the legions and centurions who had tramped along there two thousand years before. But Rebecca said:

'How very misleading to call this Stane *Street*.'

'Why?' asked Roy.

'A street usually has pavements and shops, or at least houses on either side.'

'Roman roads are always called streets' — Holly hastened to air her knowledge — 'whether they have pavements and houses or not.'

'I should have thought you would have had enough of streets to last you a lifetime,' put in Clive.

'Oh, I wasn't complaining. This bridle-path is grand, and they can call it anything they like so long as it keeps clear of the towns.'

It was incongruous to think of pavements and street lighting in connection with this lonely bridle-path running up and down through wild rough woods. A squirrel leaped across in front, springing lightly from one slender branch to the next, and a sparrow-hawk swooping over some bushes turned on the wing almost in their faces. Yet there was a subtle difference between this path and others along which they had ridden, in its amazing straightness, sweeping on regardless of the contours, and in the ancient look of the turf, in places worn thin over the bones of the hills.

After a good mile of woodland and bushes the Roman road carried them out into open country over ridges of treeless downs. They had not realized how high above the world they had climbed until they saw the farms so far below in the valley that they looked like models set out by a child amid the billows of a green quilt. It was exhilarating to canter along here on the roof of the world with only the singing larks between them and heaven. Even Crumpet recovered from the toil of the hill climbing and flew along with the rest, his forelock blown straight back between his little ears. When at last they pulled up at the cross tracks Roy said:

'Isn't it nearly time for some grub?'

'We can buy some food at that place Noel mentioned in the valley,' said Holly.

'Do you know what day it is?' asked Rebecca.

'Haven't the foggiest.'

'Sunday, and nothing will be open.'

This information was received with dismay.

'Have you got any food left from yesterday?' asked Roy faintly.

'The fag end of a loaf, some damp biscuits, and a smudge of butter.'

'Let's eat what we've got now,' said Holly in resigned tones. 'At any rate it's a lovely view.'

So they tethered the horses to some thorn bushes, and ate the scanty meal with their feet overhanging the farms in the valley. The last crumbs soon vanished, and they watched with envy the horses nibbling the short sweet cowslip-sprinkled grass. They had taken the saddles off to cool their backs, and this was a lucky move, for on Crumpet deciding to have a roll, the other three promptly copied him.

It was a long slope down to the south, and some of the pathway was stony. As they went down Rebecca began to worry over Baynard.

'I believe Gordon was right; he *is* favouring that off fore.'

'He seems to go a bit short where it's stony. Perhaps he bruised the sole yesterday,' said Roy.

'Oh dear, I do hope it's nothing really wrong! First his saddle, and then his knees, and now his foot.'

Rebecca dismounted and they all examined Baynard's foot and felt his leg, but could detect nothing amiss. This interest in him made Baynard self-conscious so that he drooped his head and dangled the leg limply. Lower in the valley the going became softer, and he threw off his look of suffering and trotted on without the suspicion of a limp. They quickly came to the tiny village so hidden in the valley that it seemed forgotten by the rest of the world.

After this they rode for a short way along Fairmile Bottom, and then crossed over into some steep woods through which Roy said there was a path to Arundel that avoided the main road. The path branched repeatedly, and they soon lost all sense of direction. Deep valleys full of beeches and horse-chestnuts and smelling damply of leaf-mould, clearings amid tangled coppice, thickets of sweet chestnut and hazel, and hushed groves of ghostly fir-trees succeeded one another without bringing the riders in sight of a cottage, let alone the little town of Arundel.

'I suppose you know where you're taking us?' said Rebecca without conviction.

'I thought I did,' confessed Roy. 'But it's so jolly difficult not being able to see more than a few yards ahead. I'll get out the compass; Arundel ought to be to the south-east.'

'What help's that if you don't know what point of the compass we're at ourselves?'

Just then Holly gave a shout:

'I've found a lot of hoof-prints down this path. They're bound to bring us either to a road or a house.'

As time was getting on they decided to follow the prints, but they had not gone far when Clive said:

'That horse-chestnut with the big branch torn off looks awfully familiar.'

'Do you know what!' exclaimed Roy, scanning the hoof-prints more closely. 'These are our own tracks!'

'People lost in jungles go round in circles,' said Clive.

'We should have kept to the compass from the start,' said Roy. 'Now for better or for worse we shall have to strike out a line and keep to it.'

'Hark, there's somebody coming!' said Holly, who was in the rear.

As they turned in their saddles to listen a small black horse burst into sight through the trees. His rider, a girl, was trying to pull up, but the horse had his head down, boring on the bit and nearly pulling her over his neck. When he saw the horses blocking the path up went his head and he halted in a few strides. The girl promptly kicked her feet out of the stirrups and jumping to the ground seized the bit with both hands. The black horse trampled in a circle, tossing his head angrily and nearly lifting her off her feet.

'Oh, don't do that!' cried Holly, jumping off too, and catching the black horse's rein, while Crumpet was left to look after himself.

The girl seemed only too glad to let someone else take charge. Directly she released her grasp on the bit the horse stopped tossing his head and began to nibble the leaves off a bush.

'I'll never get on him again!' she exclaimed.

'Then how are you going to get home?' inquired Roy.

'I don't care. I'll walk, even though it's miles.'

'Aren't you rather young to be out alone on such a strong horse?' asked Rebecca.

'I'm not young, I'm nearly fourteen! It's not my fault I'm small for my age,' came the swift retort.

The girl was no taller than Clive and slimly built. Although some of the colour had come back into her small face she looked delicate and her dishevelled golden-red hair was of the fine wispy sort. Her mud-spattered clothes were of good quality and fitted her well. Suddenly aware of their stares she blushed and said:

'I know I look a fright, but I've been simply torn through the woods, and I've lost my velvet cap.'

'Then we'd better go back and look for it, because they cost a lot,' said Rebecca.

'Oh, no! It's miles back, and I don't know which path I was on.'

'Where do you live?' asked Clive.

'Right on the other side of Arundel, across the river.'

'Oh, then you can show us the way because that's where we want to go,' said Roy, putting away the compass a shade reluctantly.

'But if you're going to walk it'll take ages, ' said Clive. 'Wouldn't your horse stay with ours all right?'

'I'm just not going to get on him again. I've tried and tried to master him, and just as I think he's going to be good something excites him and he gallops off with me. He's carried me down some simply dreadful places on the downs, so I thought in the woods where it's not so open he'd be better, but he was as bad as ever, and mummy will be furious because she thinks I ought to be such a good rider.'

The girl looked on the verge of tears, and they all felt sorry for her as she stood twisting her fingers and biting her lips.

'I know,' said Holly. 'I'll ride your horse and you can have my pony, Crumpet, who's terribly well behaved.'

'But it may gallop off with *you*,' objected Rebecca.

'I'm sure he'll keep with the others all right,' insisted Holly, who was dying to ride the black horse.

'I was going to suggest that she could ride him herself if I led her beside Baynard.'

'Some of the paths are awfully narrow, and trees have fallen across in some places,' said the girl.

'I think Holly's plan is best, but I'll ride the black, and she can have Sarah if she promises not to pull at her mouth,' said Roy.

'Oh no you don't! I thought of the swap first.'

In the end Holly had her way, and the girl, who said her name was Cynthia, got on Crumpet, who had been quietly standing unattended. Holly let down the stirrups and went to mount the black, but directly she put her toe in the iron he began to spin in circles.

'He always does that unless somebody holds him,' said Cynthia. 'Even if I'd stopped to get my cap I could never have got on again.'

Rebecca managed to hold the black horse's head just long

enough for Holly to reach the saddle. He arched his neck and danced along the path in front of the others.

'What's his name?' shouted Holly, enjoying herself.

'Ebony. Ebo for short, when he's good. Look out, not that path! The one to the right.'

Some of the paths, as she had foretold, were narrow and in places blocked by fallen trees. For all his keenness Holly found that her new mount was clever in getting by awkward places, seeming to know what he could bound over and what it was necessary to go round. Cynthia, on the other hand, was delighted with Crumpet's careful creeping and nimbleness in avoiding everything that looked the least bit dangerous. As her confidence returned she began to chatter and ask questions about her new companions and their mounts. She was amazed when she learnt how far they had come, and went into rhapsodies on discovering that Crumpet was a real Forest pony.

'My old pony, Dandy, came from Dartmoor. He's a good bit smaller than Crumpet, but with the same sort of cleverness.'

'Why don't you ride him instead of Ebony?' asked Clive.

'Well, you see, he's very old, and he goes lame after being ridden a little way. So mummy bought me Ebony because she thought I'd like one with more life in him.'

'He's certainly got life. He's as bad as Alaska,' said Rebecca.

'Alaska's not bad!' retorted Clive. 'Only keen. And this ride's done her an awful lot of good.'

'I've made myself ride Ebony every day since we've had him, and he's only got worse,' declared Cynthia. 'Oh dear, mummy is going to be cross!'

She lapsed for a while into silent misery.

The path now became broader and with a hard gritty surface that slowed Baynard down. Then Arundel appeared through the trees, the roofs and spires climbing a steep slope beyond beds of dark green water-cress. A gateway brought them out on to the high road.

'We have to go through the middle of the town to get over the Arun,' said Roy, who had brought out his map again.

'Where are you going after that?' asked Cynthia.

'Only to the youth hostel. But first we've got to find a place for the horses.'

'Oh, but we live not very far from there. I wonder if mummy would let you put them in our field. I know, I'll tell her how you saved my life – she couldn't refuse to have them then.'

'Does your mother ride?' asked Clive.

'No. I wish she did, then she'd know how difficult it can be sometimes.'

'That's just like my people,' sighed Clive.

'Does Ebony mind traffic?' inquired Holly.

'He doesn't mind it a bit – that's one of his good points.'

Arundel was small but very steep, and busy while it lasted. They came cautiously in single file down under the great castle wall to where the Arun flowed in swift coils. Once over the bridge they were soon out in the country again.

'We shouldn't be far from the hostel now,' said Roy.

'We're not. But first of all do come home with me. And perhaps *you* could explain to mummy how awful Ebony was.'

'What will you do about him?' asked Holly.

'I hope he'll be sold. But I'm so afraid that mummy won't let me have another one. You see, he was chosen by a friend of hers who's supposed to know all about horses, and he seemed quite all right when I tried him, but it was only up and down a cart track. And now they'll say it's me who's made him bad and he's not worth so much. If only I had a nice, clever, sensible pony like your Crumpet I'd go in for jumping and gymkhanas like I did on Dandy.'

'Do you really like Crumpet?' asked Holly with a glint of inspiration in her eye.

'I think he's lovely. He's so kind and gentle, and doesn't keep jerking at my arms and throwing me about in the saddle, and yet I'm sure he'd go fast if I asked him to.'

'Oh, yes, he's quite fast for his size, and he can jump too. You wouldn't like to change, would you?'

'What, me have Crumpet and you have Ebony?' cried Cynthia, while Rebecca, Roy, and Clive gaped. 'Oh, I would! I'd simply love it!'

'But you can't do that, Holly,' broke in Rebecca. 'Whatever would uncle say?'

'He said I could sell Crumpet and get a bigger one. This is almost the same thing without bothering about money.'

'I know, but he didn't mean you were to swap Crumpet for a horse he's never even set eyes on. Why, you don't know anything about Ebony except that he bolts – how old he is, or whether he's sound or not.'

'Oh, I can tell you all about him,' Cynthia said hastily. 'He's by a thoroughbred out of a Fell pony – that's on the certificate – and he's nine years old, and the vet passed him as sound before we got him. You can see it all in writing at home.'

'There you are!' said Holly triumphantly. 'What do you think about it, Roy?'

'He looks a topper,' said Roy. 'But dad mightn't let you keep him of course.'

'It's worth the risk, Holly,' urged Clive. 'I think he's a beaut, and full of spirit, just like Alaska.'

'Perhaps Cynthia's mother won't agree. A fifteen-hand horse is worth a lot more than a thirteen-two pony,' said Rebecca hopefully.

'He's not worth anything to Cynthia if she won't ride him. And Crumpet is three years younger, so he's got that advantage over Ebony, and Cynthia's not a bit too big for him, so he'll last her several years.'

'Well, here we are – this is my home,' said Cynthia. 'I can see mummy in the garden. Oh, I do wonder what she'll say!'

She led them up a drive to an ivy-clad house. A tall thin lady who had been digging a flower bed left her fork standing and came to meet them.

'Why, what's all this? Why's that girl riding Ebony?'

'Oh, mummy, mummy, they've saved my life! They have really. Ebony bolted again, and if they hadn't stopped him in the woods he'd have carried me right out on to the road the rate he was going. And I've lost my cap, and this nice girl, Holly, has let me ride back on her own darling Crumpet, who's absolutely safe.'

'You silly child, I told you not to let Ebony get into a gallop.'

'But I don't think she could stop him,' pleaded Holly. 'He's awfully headstrong, you know.'

'And so you stopped him for her. Well, it was very kind of you, I'm sure. But who are you? I don't think I have met any of you before?'

'We're on a riding tour, and we really ought to be going on our way,' said Rebecca, anxious to remove Holly before she got herself involved.

'A riding tour! Now that is a nice thing to do. Why don't you do that with one of your friends, Cynthia?'

'I'd simply love to if only I could manage Ebony.'

'I think he's a bit big for her,' said Roy politely, with an eye to furthering Holly's plan.

'Yes, so do I,' piped up Clive. 'Cynthia's no bigger than me, while Ebony's much taller than Alaska, and I'm a boy too.'

'Well, I hoped she'd grow into Ebony,' sighed Cynthia's mother. 'What a nuisance it is. It's going to be a job to sell him locally now. We'll have to hire a pony by the hour. I really can't go through all this trouble of buying a pony again.'

'Mummy, you won't have to do that. Holly's quite willing to exchange Crumpet for Ebony, and Crumpet would be simply wonderful for me, 'cos he's so obedient and clever, and they say he can jump, and he's only six.'

'Which one's Crumpet?'

'Why, this darling one I'm on. He fits me beautifully.'

'He's a real Forest pony,' said Holly. 'We know it's true because we bought him in the Forest, and you can tell by the notch in his tail which part he belongs to.'

'Well, they do say native ponies are so safe, and certainly Dandy was,' said the mother. 'But wait a minute, this is rushing things too much. I can't decide a thing like this straight off. We should have to talk it over with my friend Mr Cuthbert. Must you go just yet?'

'We're only going to the youth hostel,' said Roy.

'Yes, and, mummy, couldn't they leave their horses for the night in the field?' added Cynthia. 'You know Mr Cuthbert said it ought to be grazed down 'cos with only two horses the grass will run away.'

'Well, yes, I suppose that would be all right. Do you want to leave them now?'

'Yes, please,' said Holly promptly, in case Rebecca should turn the idea down. 'They've come a long way.'

'Where have you come from today?'

'Goodwood.'

'Oh, that's a long way away!' Cynthia's mother looked at them with increased respect. 'Show them the field, Cynthia, and in the meantime we shall have to think over this horse business.'

'I believe she will agree in the end,' chirruped Cynthia as she led them off. 'She wasn't half so cross as I'd feared, and I'm sure she realizes that you're awfully good riders and know heaps about horses.'

Rebecca gave a derisive snort at this last remark. Although glad that they had found a field for the horses so quickly, she was not at all happy about the rest of the proceedings.

When the horses were all turned out together there was a certain amount of curiosity shown over Ebony. Sarah could not make up her mind whether the black horse was more handsome than Baynard, and while she made advances to him she kept a wary eye on Alaska in case she should usurp her old favourite. These manoeuvres caused a good deal of circling and snorting, Crumpet being careful to keep on the outskirts.

'Old Dandy doesn't know he's got visitors yet,' said Cynthia. 'Oh, here he comes!'

The retired Dartmoor pony came trotting stiffly across the field, and whinnied piercingly like the ponies in the Forest. He took a quick survey of the others, then trotted up to Crumpet and smelt noses with him. A kick, or at least a squeal, seemed imminent; then, as if recognizing kindred spirits, the two little native ponies fell to nibbling one another's manes.

'There, you see, they're friends at once!' said Holly. 'They'd love to live together always.'

'Oh, they must! It would never do to part them now.' Cynthia had already made up her mind about it.

11

Holly does a deal

THE youth hostel was a big stone house hidden behind an avenue of limes. An empty conservatory covering the front door echoed to the tramp of hikers' boots, and inside the evening shadows were gathering along the passages and stairways. The warden was nonplussed when he heard that the four had arrived on horseback, for in his register of hostellers there were only three headings under which to enter their modes of travel.

'You're not canoeists or cyclists,' he said sadly. 'Could you possibly describe yourselves as walkers?'

'We've walked up from where we've left the horses,' said Rebecca helpfully.

'And I've walked up most of the hills to save my pony,' added Holly.

'Walkers will do,' said the warden with finality. 'Perhaps one day they'll add a column for horsemen.'

He gave them their sleeping-bags and told them the numbers of their rooms, which they found with some difficulty in the rambling upper storey. At last Holly and Rebecca found their beds in a huge room so closely stacked with two-tier bunks that it resembled the left luggage department of a railway station.

'My turn to sleep on top,' said Holly.

'Then for heaven's sake don't shake about in the night,' said Rebecca, tossing her bag on the lower bunk. She was still worried over Holly's plan of changing the pony, and spoke shortly.

Several girls were busy making up their beds, and French and Scandinavian were spoken in the general chatter. Just outside the door a back stair led down into the room where hostellers described as 'self-cooking' prepared their own meals, and from which now arose a very savoury smell of frying.

'Oh, I hope they give us a big supper,' said Holly. 'The view from Bignor Hill was splendid, but the lunch was a wash-out!'

After washing in tepid water they hastened down to the canteen. Roy and Clive were already there, helping to hand round bowls of steaming soup. They took their places at the long tables with a dozen or so others, all equally hungry. No one spoke much until the soup was gone, and then conversation started up as walkers and cyclists began to compare notes on the day's travels. Two young men said they had cycled from London that day, and on the next hoped to get to the Isle of Wight.

'How many miles can you do a day?' asked Clive.

'Ninety odd,' replied one nonchalantly. 'It's no good standing still, you know.'

'That's like Cecil,' said Holly. 'We might meet him at a hostel one day.'

'I hope we don't,' said Roy. 'What about my ferrets?'

After supper they took a last look at the horses for the night. Holly had eyes for none but the black horse, Ebony. She studied him from all angles. He was not big enough for a point-to-point – she could see that at once – but anyhow interfering grown-ups would probably have said she was too young to ride in one. On the other hand he was decidedly a step up from Crumpet, and so much younger and more lively than Kelly; his coat was so black and sleek and his white socks so very white and his tail literally swept the grass. When he put his nose gently against her hand and peered at her with a humorous look in his large eyes as if they shared a private joke, she made up her mind not to leave Arundel until she had done everything in her power to bring about the exchange.

While they were in the field Cynthia and her mother came out, and Cynthia lost no time in pointing out what fast friends Crumpet and Dandy had already become. Her mother sounded quite worn out by Cynthia's talk, and clung to one statement:

'We'll have to see what Mr Cuthbert says.'

'But he won't be here until tomorrow, and then they'll be gone!'

'He's coming over in the morning about eleven. Couldn't you possibly stay till then?' her mother asked the others.

'Of course we could,' said Holly, but even Roy looked dubious, although he was on her side.

'It's a long way to Patcham, the next hostel,' he said. 'A lot of it's across country, too, so there's just a chance of losing the way now and then.'

'If you could stop another night we could keep the horses.'

'Couldn't we do that, Rebecca?' implored Holly. 'I'm sure all the horses need a bit of a rest.'

'Oh, well, stay if you're all so set on it,' replied Rebecca. 'And let's hope this Mr Cuthbert will put his foot on the whole hare-brained scheme. You'll probably believe a complete stranger, and at any rate you won't be nagging at me for the rest of the way home.'

'Then we'll stay,' said Holly, unabashed by her cousin's irritation.

They returned in the twilight, and gathered with the other hostellers round a fine glowing fire that the warden had lit for them in the common-room, for the evening had turned chilly. A row of damp boots and shoes steamed round the kerb, and the sight of various people scribbling messages to their friends and relations at home reminded the riders that they ought to buy some more postcards next day. Two fair-haired girls, who had cooked their own suppers, joined the group. They wore shirts patterned in bold checks and the briefest possible shorts, and the moment they spoke every one knew they were from either America or Canada.

'Say, weren't you the folks we saw crossing over Fairmile Bottom on horseback?' one asked Roy.

'Why, yes, and it was you who came down on bikes?'

'Sure, we were the guys, and weren't we just envious of you! I said to Anita here: "Let's get shut of these pedal outfits and get ourselves a couple of horses".'

'And I told her our vacation wouldn't last that long if we

were going to see Canterbury Cathedral and Edinburgh Castle as we'd planned,' broke in Anita. 'But you folks ought to come to Canada and ride through the Rockies.'

Later, while they were going to bed, Holly took advantage of Rebecca's improved temper to say :

'I can't think why you're so dead against my doing a chop with Cynthia. Daddy definitely said I could sell him and get a bigger one, which comes to the same thing.'

'And I've already told you that he didn't mean you to do it off your own bat. If this black horse turns out to be a wrong 'un the money he paid for Crumpet will just go down the drain.'

'Well, that would be my loss, and I should still have old Kelly. But how could anything be wrong with Ebony when he was passed by the vet only a few weeks ago?'

'It's not only soundness, but temperament. This habit of bolting madly off might land you in a nasty jam one day.'

'Oh, but I'm much bigger and stronger than Cynthia, who obviously just loses her head every time she thinks he's going a bit spare. And another thing, she rides him on a plain curb with a port and a chain and only one rein.'

'Well, that's a very severe bit, and it still doesn't control him.'

'I know, but I've read lots of horse books, and they all say that a curb lowers a horse's head. Ebony was boring badly, and I believe if he had a snaffle he'd hold his head up and be more easily stopped.'

'Can't you two stop jawing,' grumbled a muffled voice from a nearby bed. 'Some people here want to sleep.'

Abashed, they crept into bed, the bunk creaking and swaying as Holly climbed on top.

They awoke to the monotonous sound of water finding its own level. Morning had come in with scudding rain clouds. The angle of slate roof opposite their window gleamed dully, and in the field below a herd of cows stood disconsolately with their backs to the wind. Most of the other hostellers found it necessary to push on. In ones and twos they departed, muffled in crackling green or yellow oilskins. Last to go were the two Canadian girls.

'So long, see you in the Rockies!' they called to the riders as they bowled away down the drive.

At about eleven the rain lessened to a fine wind-blown mist, and a watery light shone upon wet leaves and walls. Rebecca suddenly announced that she was going to take Baynard to the forge in the town.

'Why, does he want new shoes?' asked Roy.

'No, but I want the smith to move the front ones and see if he can find anything wrong with that foot.'

She went off on Baynard without saying a word more about the proposed exchange. Holly suspected that she had chosen to be out of the way on purpose. Although this gave Holly a free hand, she began to experience a slight qualm. It was a pretty drastic thing she was contemplating, and it would have been much less alarming done with her cousin's help and approval. Although Roy supported her, he was only a year older, and Clive, of course, was quite a kid. She began to wonder exactly what her father would say if she arrived home with a strange black horse of dubious character instead of the reliable pony he had bought for her.

When they went along to Cynthia's house she ran out to meet them.

'I didn't sleep a wink last night for fear you'd be gone in the morning after all. Mr Cuthbert has rung up to say he'll be along as soon as it's stopped raining, so we'd better catch Crumpet.'

The rain-sleeked Crumpet was brought into the garage to wait. At last a car drove up and a short fat man got out. This was Mr Cuthbert.

'What's all this about changing the horse we chose for you, Cynthia?' he asked sternly. 'What's wrong with him?'

Cynthia hung her head, her eloquence failing her.

'There's nothing really wrong with Ebony,' said her mother, who had come out, 'except that Cynthia can't seem to stop him.'

'But she'll learn with time.'

'I dare say, but she's already lost her whip on the downs, and now her new velvet cap in the woods. If she's going to lose something every time he runs away it'll cost me pounds. And now these young people have turned up with a pony which they're willing to exchange for Ebony, and Cynthia seems rather to have fallen for it.'

'What she needs is a rocking-horse,' snapped Mr Cuthbert. 'Is this the pony?'

'He's a very good pony,' said Holly, thinking it was time she said something. 'He carries Cynthia beautifully, and she wants to ride him in gymkhanas.'

'Forest pony, I hear,' said Mr Cuthbert. 'Nothing wrong in that. Nice shoulders and legs, and well put together, but small. Let's see you ride him, Cynthia.'

Cynthia mounted and rode Crumpet up and down the drive. They made an attractive and well-matched pair.

'I must say Cynthia does look happier and safer,' remarked her mother. 'Perhaps Ebony is a bit big for her. She has such a job getting on. What do you think, Mr Cuthbert?'

Before committing himself further Mr Cuthbert performed the traditional rites of feeling Crumpet's fine little legs, picking up his hoofs, and opening his mouth. Crumpet submitting with good grace. The verdict was slow and weighty.

'I can't fault him. But of course he's nothing like so smart as Ebony, though rather more temperate. What was the basis of the exchange.'

'A real swap,' broke in Cynthia.

'But Ebony is worth more than the pony.'

'Oh, but our Crumpet is three years younger and much better trained,' Roy put in.

'Yes, he's been properly schooled, and goes collectedly in all his paces,' said Holly, quoting one of Mrs Holland's phrases.

'Ebony's got no manners at all,' said Clive grandly, as if he owned the best-mannered pony in the world.

'I'm sure he had. Cynthia must have spoilt them. I think it would be quite in order to ask for ten pounds and the pony in return for Ebony.'

'Oh, but we couldn't do that!' exclaimed Holly. 'We haven't got ten pounds.'

Her chance of owning Ebony was fading, and all because of this silly interfering man. But Cynthia here interposed forcefully.

'You can't ask them for ten pounds after they've saved my life, and now wasted a whole day of their holidays. You just couldn't, mummy! And if we keep Ebony I'll never ride him again, ever, so he'll just be a complete dead loss, because I shall tell every one how awful he is, and no one will want to buy him.'

The appeal to her sense of gratitude combined with the final masterly threat quite overcame Cynthia's mother.

'I hate haggling,' she said. 'So long as you say the pony is quite all right, Mr Cuthbert, I'm satisfied. All I ask is that you go for a ride this afternoon and look for the lost cap; that cost nearly five pounds.'

For good or ill Holly had got her black horse.

12

Second thoughts

REBECCA came back from the forge in a much better temper.

'We've found out the cause of Baynard's trouble,' she said. 'It was only a corn. The smith cut it out and put back the shoe, and now the old horse trots completely sound again. Am I relieved! And I've bought some postcards for you, and something for lunch. As it's turned out fine I thought we could have a picnic by the river.'

The others were equally glad to hear the news about Baynard.

'That kid Gordon was pretty sharp, wasn't he?' said Clive.

Rebecca did not inquire how they had got on with Mr Cuthbert, and nobody liked to risk upsetting her good humour by telling her what had happened. They went down to the river bank and chose a good spot for their meal while talking of other things.

Although Holly's thoughts were running riot over her new possession their surroundings made an impression upon her. The distant castle rising across the green levels, the swift river, and the rustling sedges full of chattering sedge-warblers for a long time remained connected in her mind with the lively black horse.

'And what's to do this afternoon?' Rebecca's voice broke in upon her thoughts. 'I want to give Baynard the rest of the day off.'

'I don't think Alaska really needs a rest,' said Clive. 'Can I come with you, Holly, when you ride with Cynthia?'

'Oh, so you're already fixed up,' said Rebecca in a strange-sounding voice.

'Well, yes, we're going back to those woods to look for Cynthia's cap,' said Holly. Then, knowing that the position would have to be made clear before long: 'You see, we've done the swap. Cynthia's keeping Crumpet and I'm having Ebony.'

She tried unsuccessfully to keep a note of defiance out of her voice. Rebecca's face remained impassive, but her reply was shattering.

'Then you'd better unswap quickly. I phoned up your father while I was in Arundel.'

'Rebecca!'

All three shot bolt upright and stared at her.

'But that's sneaking!' exclaimed Clive.

'It isn't. And anyhow it's nothing to do with you,' retorted Rebecca, showing the first signs of emotion.

'What did daddy say?' demanded Holly. 'I bet you made Ebony sound much worse than he is on purpose'

'No I didn't. I said he was good-looking and as far as any one could be sure quite sound, but that he was wild and badly trained and accustomed to bolt with his other rider, which is all perfectly true.'

'What did he say to that?'

'That I was to do everything in my power to persuade you against having him.'

'Then he didn't say outright I wasn't to have Ebony?'

'No. But he did say that if you persisted in bringing the horse home he made no promise at all that you could keep him. If he didn't think Ebony was safe for you he'd have to be sent to the very next sale and sold just for what he'll fetch. So you'd run the risk of losing nearly all the money paid for Crumpet.'

'My word, that's some gamble, Hol!' exclaimed Roy. 'What will you do now?'

Holly gazed at the hurrying waters and wished the sedge-warblers would be quiet so that she could think more clearly. At last she announced:

'I shall ride Ebony this afternoon as we arranged, and decide after that.'

'I don't see how you could back out now that it's all settled,' said Clive, risking another rebuff.

'No, nor do I really,' agreed Holly. 'You should have phoned up last night, Rebecca, if you were bent on interfering.'

'If there's nothing in writing they can't hold you to it.'

'But it would be pretty mean,' said Roy.

'Would you rather Holly had a bad accident, or lose her chance of getting a decent horse just for fear of offending some perfect strangers? Cynthia would be no worse off than before we met her.'

'I suppose there's something in what you say,' conceded Roy, pulled in two directions.

'Well, it's entirely my business, and it's me who's going to decide,' said Holly. 'So kindly stop talking about me as if I wasn't here!'

The picnic broke up on this rather stormy note. Holly and Clive went off to ride with Cynthia, leaving Rebecca and Roy to their own devices. Holly's heart was sore not only with conflict over Crumpet and Ebony, but also because she felt Roy was on the verge of siding with Rebecca. It was a turning of the tables to find a staunch ally in Clive.

'Don't you give in to them,' he said. 'I'd risk everything in the world for Ebony if I were you.'

As Crumpet could wear old Dandy's snaffle bridle Holly used her own on Ebony. This fitted him much better than it did Crumpet. Kelly's saddle also rode better on Ebony than it had on Crumpet's short back.

'I think you're awfully brave to ride him in a snaffle,' said Cynthia as they set out. 'The people we bought him from rode him in a pelham, but I hate having two reins.'

All went well along the road and through the town. Ebony walked briskly, nodding his head and not attempting to pull, although now and then he clinked the bit reflectively. Once in the woods he broke into a springy jog, pricking his ears to and fro and peering mischievously back at Holly, but with his head well up she felt she had him under control.

'I'll try to remember exactly where I went yesterday,' said Cynthia. 'We'd better not go too fast in case we gallop over my cap.'

While Ebony and Alaska bounded along the rides in some excitement, Crumpet behaved much more sedately with Cynthia. But it was Alaska who first spotted the cap, shying away from it under the impression that it was something dangerous.

"Fraid it's a bit muddy,' said Clive.

'Never mind,' said Cynthia, giving it a rub with her sleeve and clapping it on her head. 'I hated it for looking so new.'

After this she said she knew a way through the park where Holly could give Ebony a better trial. Holly, whose notion of a park was a flat bit of turf with some big trees growing in it, was astonished not only by the size of this one, but by the steepness of its hills, which were a continuation of the downs.

A long stretch of turf tempted Holly to test Ebony's speed. Ebony was more than willing to oblige, and no sooner did he find Alaska blowing and straining beside him than he redoubled his efforts. They reached the end of the level ground much too soon, and seeing a downward stretch before them Holly stuck her knees hard into the saddle flaps and tried to pull up. But she had left it too late. Faster and faster they went down the hill towards the gleam of water between tree trunks at the bottom, the gallop becoming a scrambling slide.

In a panic Holly tugged and sawed at the snaffle until her arms ached. Ebony threw up his head and seemed trying to dig in his hind hoofs, but the hill had now become so steep that he was unable to stop himself. He turned sharply under the trees, where Holly was partly blinded by twigs, and then halted in a few paces, causing her to bang her nose against the back of his neck. When she could see again she found they were standing by a swing gate which Ebony, by his impatient glances round, evidently expected her to open. Alaska came slithering down the hill not very far behind, and then at a good distance in the rear appeared Crumpet, picking his way briskly but delicately down.

'I say, I thought you meant to jump that gate!' exclaimed Clive.

'Perhaps my snaffle idea wasn't so good after all,' confessed Holly. 'He seems able to go just as fast with his head up.'

'I think he had it up too high. A martingale might keep it just right. And of course the downhill came almost before we thought about pulling up.'

'Ooh, you're all right then? Did you mean to go as fast as that down there?' asked Cynthia, coming up with them. 'Ooh, I'm jolly glad it wasn't me! I say, you won't want Crumpet back now, will you?'

This was the very line along which Holly's mind was working. She had been really frightened during the career downhill. Although Kelly had a hard mouth, shortness of wind had always prevented him from getting out of control, and this feeling of utter helplessness was something new to her. Avoiding Cynthia's imploring eyes and Clive's rather inquisitive stare, she bent down to unlatch the gate. Ebony opened it for her with a well-timed thrust, and strode through.

'Well, why don't you say something?' urged Cynthia, after they had shut the gate.

'Are you afraid of him?' asked Clive. 'It feels a bit funny not always being able to stop, but you get used to it.'

'Of course I'm not afraid,' said Holly, remembering the argument with Mrs Holland over the joys of galloping. 'I was just thinking of what you said about martingales. I wonder if we could get one in Arundel.'

'Oh, yes, there's a saddler there,' said Cynthia eagerly. 'We can pass him on the way home. Oh, thank goodness I can keep Crumpet!'

Half of Holly wanted to say, 'No, you can't; I want Crumpet back.' But the other half, partly made up of pride, stifled the words. It was not only fear of what the others might say that kept her from speaking; in spite of her scare she was still genuinely attracted by Ebony's gay spirit. He's got a good heart, she told herself. I'm sure he'd never do anything mean. And he does seem able to look after himself while he's tearing along.

A track beside a lake brought them into Arundel. But when she went into the saddler's shop she found that a martingale would cost over a guinea.

'Is that the cheapest?' she exclaimed.

'Good leather is expensive these days, miss,' said the saddler. 'But wait a minute.' He rummaged in the back of the shop and produced a second-hand one. 'It's a bit shabby and been mended but it's quite sound. Ten shillings to you, miss.'

Holly counted out four half-crowns, and noted with sorrow that her store was dwindling. Remembering that she still owed Rebecca for postcards and her share of lunch, she realized that she would have to economize during the rest of the ride.

Walking back from Cynthia's house to the hostel she said to Clive:

'Don't say anything to Rebecca, or even Roy just yet, about Ebony dashing down that hill.'

'Of course not. Cut my throat,' said Clive, impressed at being treated as a conspirator. 'I think Ebony's tophole, and I'm sure your father will too, if only you can cure him of bolting before you get home.'

'If only I can,' agreed Holly.

'Well, look how much better Alaska's got on this ride. She hasn't bolted off once since we left the Forest, or done any real bucks, either.'

'Hallo,' said Roy, when they met at supper. 'Got back all in one piece?'

'Of course. And Ebony's even better than Crumpet at opening gates.'

'Does that mean you've really decided to keep him?' asked Rebecca. 'Well, it's not my responsibility any more, though I think you're an ass. Did he –'

'We found Cynthia's cap all right.' Clive cut across the threatened question with a sharpness that filled Holly with admiration. 'Her mother wasn't half glad.'

'Yes, and she's promised us some hard-boiled ducks' eggs tomorrow to take with us for lunch,' Holly went on quickly.

'That's about the best thing that's come out of our stay here,' remarked Rebecca.

On the following morning it was raining again, but they

could not stay another day, and went down to the field to saddle the wet horses.

'I bet Crumpet's glad he's staying behind,' said Roy, as they fumbled with slippery buckles and straps while the horses fidgeted irritably. Wrapped in waterproofs, Cynthia and her mother saw them off, wishing them luck and Holly success with Ebony. Ebony disliked the rain. With his tail clamped down and his ears back he bore no resemblance to the gay horse of the previous day. They scrambled up on to damp saddles and started off along the lane. Crumpet and Dandy trotted along inside the hedge whinnying good-bye. Holly felt a pang when she looked for the last time on Crumpet's sharp little pony face with the raindrops beading his long lashes like tears. His was an endearing personality, and at this moment she felt more acutely than ever the risk she was taking. Her only consolation just then was that Crumpet had a good home, a nice companion in old Dandy, and a mistress who adored him from the start.

'We've got a long way to go today,' remarked Roy rather gloomily. 'This should bring us through Wepham Woods, and then we go over the downs to Findon.'

'Wettam Woods, I guess,' said Rebecca, but her pun fell flat.

However, a brisk trot up the path through the woods warmed them up, the horses began to steam, and life did not look quite so grey. The wood was full of rich mushroomy scents released by the rain, and when they brushed through the last screen of wet leaves and came out on the downs they found that the wind had blown the clouds up into scattered heaps and blue sky was shining through.

They were on a ridge which ran, level as a racecourse, high above the next valley, in which nestled a lonely farm. The horses' hoofs scattered the raindrops from grass blades and fat daisies, and the smell of mushroom was replaced by the heady fragrance of wild thyme. Ebony sensed the canter that was coming and started to bounce like a rubber ball. Wondering if their next stop would be on the roof of the farm Holly eased the rein. Away they went into the wind over the springy turf for half a mile or more. Holly was not quite certain how much control she had over Ebony during that canter, but he pulled up when the others did, and she fancied that the martingale helped to steady his more exuberant bounds.

'He does seem a trifle less wild in a snaffle and with that martingale,' Rebecca acknowledged. 'But the test will come when he's grown used to it.'

For the next few miles Roy's map-reading was unerring. He led them by tracks across the downs through Mitchel Grove, an old racing stable, and Myrtle Grove, a remote farm, and brought them triumphantly out at the big village of Findon. It was wonderful riding country, with turf all the way. Holly would have enjoyed looking round her more at the downs with their dark woods and open flower-painted slopes skimmed by swallows if she had not been so much occupied with Ebony's behaviour. This, on the whole, was good, but her very tenseness made him jumpy, so that they kept alarming each other. It was Roy who, riding up close, whispered:

'For heaven's sake relax a bit, Hol. You look as if you were sitting on a volcano that was about to erupt.'

Holly actually laughed, and did manage to relax a little after that.

At Findon they bought some brown bread and cheese to go with the eggs, and then, feeling thirsty after so much cantering, stopped at a sweet shop for bottles of brightly coloured drink. While they were swigging these in the road two smart riders passed on faultlessly turned-out horses. They stared at the travellers with some surprise. The horses were nibbling the grass off a bank. Their damp, mud-splashed coats, dulled, grass-stained bits, and smeary leather compared most unfavourably with those passing by. In addition to the bundles tied round the saddles, Sarah had a loaf balanced on hers, Baynard's bits of extra felt were poking untidily out from under his numnah, and Alaska's halter rope was looped round her neck. As for the riders, their hair was dishevelled by wind and rain, their clothes crumpled, and their shoes muddy.

The girls, having seen their reflections in the shop window,

turned the other way, but Roy, quite unabashed, stepped into
the road, bottle in hand, and asked the foremost rider :

'Excuse me, can you tell us where our horses could get a
drink?'

The man he addressed, who looked like a superior kind of
groom, shook his head and rode on, but the other, a woman,
drew up and said curiously :

'Have you come far?'

'From the New Forest.'

'Well, that really is a ride! You can water your horses in
my yard, but it's a good way up the hill.'

She was obviously impressed by the distance they had come,
but the groom continued to disapprove. As they rode on he
said to the woman :

'Tourists on horseback, ma'am. Whatever next!'

They did not go to the stable yard because the kind lady at
the shop lent them a bucket and showed them where they could
fill it from a tap. They ate their lunch on the hill just above
Findon in company with a Guernsey bull, fortunately tethered.
Baynard, Sarah, and Alaska had by now got used to feeding by
the wayside, and hardly needed to be tied up. But the routine
was new to Ebony, who tramped restlessly about on the end of
his rope, which Holly held for safety's sake, thrusting his
nose into the paper bags, and trying to nibble the grass on
which they sat.

'If you must keep that animal near you, for goodness' sake
go and sit on your own!' exclaimed Rebecca, rescuing the sausage-rolls in the nick of time. 'He's a perfect menace at meal
time.'

Holly sighed and removed herself and Ebony farther away.

'She's not even trying to like you, Ebo.'

Ebony did not look unduly disturbed at this piece of news.

13

Country into town

BEYOND Findon the downs changed their character. There were no more big woods, and the bold contours of the hills were broken only by gorse bushes or a few ragged fir-trees, and patches of blossoming thorn-trees filled the deep denes with a drowsy scent. The white tracks and bridle-paths were visible for miles ahead, in places so steep that the going was toilsome, and here Holly began to appreciate Ebony's strong limbs and back.

'Poor little Crumpet wouldn't have cared much for these hills,' she remarked. 'I should have had to walk most of the way with him, but Ebony could leave you all behind.'

'He's fresh, while the others have been travelling a good many days now,' said Rebecca. 'Alaska was just as bouncing at the start.'

'Oh, but she could still go like anything if I wanted her to,' Clive hastened to add. 'It's only that the steady work has made her more sensible.'

'And what it's done for Alaska it'll do for Ebony,' said Holly triumphantly. 'You can't have it both ways, you see, Rebecca.'

'That's quite true. You must admit that either Ebony will always be fresh and able to keep ahead, or else he'll settle down like Alaska,' said Roy, siding with Holly again.

In fact, all three agreed that Rebecca had acted in an underhand way when she telephoned to Mr Granger without warning Holly first. Rebecca herself now realized this. She excused herself on the score that she had done it for Holly's own good, and bore the others' disapproval with an air of martyrdom that sat oddly upon her blunt and naturally cheerful disposition.

To cross the river Adur, which carved its way through the downs from the Weald of Sussex to the sea, meant the travellers coming down into Bramber, where there was a bridge. As before the horses did not take kindly to the main road running through Steyning, Bramber, and Upper Beeding, three villages strung together along the valley where it was hot and noisy with passing traffic. But up on the downs once more after a stiff climb the cool wind fanned their sweating necks and the riders' damp foreheads as they passed along a great rampart overlooking the Sussex Weald. Seeing the Weald almost just below their stirrups with the Adur flowing through it in snaky curves gave them the feeling of being much higher up than when riding through the heart of the downs. Presently they came to a dene looking as if it had been cut sharply out with a putty knife while the downs were still soft.

'How would you like to be run away with down there on Ebony?' Clive asked Holly softly.

'Much the same as you would on Alaska!'

'That,' said Roy, with the air of a conjurer producing a rabbit out of a hat, 'is the Devil's Dyke.'

'What did the devil have to do with it?' asked Holly.

'It's written on the map in fancy letters, which means it's very old.'

'Well, it certainly doesn't look as if it came here yesterday,' said Rebecca. 'What's more important, how far is it to Patcham?'

'Oh, just a few miles if we can find the right paths.'

The horses were getting hungry and kept putting down their heads to snatch tufts of grass to the discomfort of their riders.

'I wonder how long it will be before we get home,' remarked Clive suddenly.

'Funny, I was just working that out,' said Roy. 'Three days' ride at the very least.'

Strangely enough Holly too had been thinking of Haffeneys, and wondering how the people and animals there were getting on. She was on the verge of asking Rebecca if there had been any news when she rang up the day before, but a streak of pride kept her from referring to the unlucky call, and just then Clive said:

'What are those two windmills right over there?'

'Clayton mills, Jack and Jill,' said Roy. 'Patcham should be only a mile or two south of us.'

'It was only a few miles hours ago.'

'Well, we've been going more slowly.'

'There's a big red chimney in the valley,' said Holly, whom Ebony carried into the lead down the hill.

'That's right; that's the waterworks.'

'Then that must be Patcham; but, my word, it's a jolly great town!'

A sea of red roofs had come into view beyond the fall of the hill; it seemed to stretch for miles along the valley, and the hum of traffic now came clearly up to them. Consternation spread among them as they descended the long slope.

'We shall never find a field for the horses here.'

'Don't lose hope,' said Rebecca. 'We felt just the same about Chandler's Ford remember.'

The track brought them down under a railway bridge and on to a busy main road. Roy hailed two girls bicycling by with packs on their backs.

'Can you tell us the way to the youth hostel, please?'

'Just along this road, only a few hundred yards,' replied one, wearing velvet shorts and a wind jacket. 'But what are you going to do with those horses? There's nowhere at the hostel to keep them.'

'We don't quite know what to do,' said Rebecca. 'We thought Patcham would be a village with fields close to it.'

'It was not so long ago, but it's a suburb of Brighton now,' a voice said behind them. It belonged to an elderly lady with a plump brown spaniel. 'How lucky you are to have horses,' she went on. 'I used to ride on the downs in my young days. There are one or two riding schools which might put them up, but I expect they'd charge you a good bit.'

'We really want a field for them,' said Holly. 'They like that better than stables.'

'My neighbour has a little paddock at the bottom of his garden. If you like to come along with me I could ask him for you. He's only got a donkey and some fowls in it.'

The man who owned the paddock turned out to be deaf, and when the lady asked if the horses could go in with the donkey, he thought that they wanted to buy his pet.

'Won't hear of it. Old pensioner, never sell her as long as we live!' he declared loudly, banging the path with his stick. 'What you want is a pack-horse.' But on the lady persevering, he gathered what they really wanted, and began to hum and ha. 'Never had horses in here before. D'you think they'd chase my hens?'

At last he agreed to have the horses for the night. They entered the paddock by a rickety gate made out of the end of an iron bedstead, and were dismayed to find that it was very small indeed and the grass scanty and overrun by hens and nettles.

'They won't get anything to eat here,' whispered Holly. 'Whatever shall we do?'

Rebecca noticed the old lady with the spaniel beckoning from the gate, and they went to hear what she had to say.

'Buy them some porridge oats,' she hissed. 'That's what he does for his donkey, and she loves them.'

This, they agreed, seemed the best solution, and Roy was dispatched hastily to the nearest shop in case it was getting on for closing time. Immediately they were free, the horses toured the paddock, sniffing at the dirty grass and nettles with disapproving snorts. The donkey, who had been resting behind a hen house, came out to inspect them. Her sudden appearance startled the horses. They wheeled away in a bunch, and Alaska tripped over some wire netting, while hens ran cackling in all directions. The donkey began to bray threateningly, but Sarah snapped at her with her ears back, and realizing that she was heavily outnumbered she accepted them under protest. The old man told them that the donkey was over thirty years old, and used to pull his vegetable barrow before he retired. The lady admired all the horses.

'Such beautiful creatures; so sad to think that their day is nearly over.'

'Oh, but they're all quite young,' said Holly.

'Ah, but I was referring to the whole equine race : so near to extinction. Soon we shall only see them in zoos and museums.'

With this depressing notion falling upon their ears the riders opened Roy's packets of oats and distributed them in some troughs from which the hens fed. The horses rushed upon the mealy white oats, and so did the hens and the donkey to the accompaniment of squeals, stampings, and cackling which fortunately the old man was too deaf to hear. He stood by smiling, delighted that his live-stock were getting some pickings.

'You can fill that tank with water from my sink,' he said. 'It'll save me doing it myself for Jenny. And your harness can go in the woodshed. Nobody won't touch it because my ole bitch, Rosie, sleeps in there, and she's got a reputation.'

They soon sampled Rosie's reputation when with hackles up and bared yellow teeth she flew at them for the length of her chain which was fastened to the woodshed door.

'Better leave it on the ground and I'll put it away when you've gone,' said Rosie's master, regarding her choking efforts to get at the visitors with pride.

Feeling that they had done the best they could for the horses they gathered up their bags and went to find the youth hostel. This was a tall stately house set in green turf and flanked by big rook-haunted trees. Their lodgings seemed so grand compared with the dingy paddock that they felt sorrier for the horses than ever. They were only just in time for supper.

'Did you get a place for the horses?' asked the girl in velvet shorts, who was sitting at the same table.

'We got them a place, and that's about all you can say for it,' replied Rebecca.

'Brighton's a funny place to choose to come with horses. Most people come for the beach and the entertainments.'

'But this isn't Brighton on the map,' objected Roy crossly.

'Near enough to make no difference,' said a sunburnt young

man with a peeling nose. 'First-class place, Brighton. Coming down tonight to the fun fair? They've got some smashing dodgems.'

'Ooh, yes, let's go. I love dodgems!' cried Clive.

'You can keep them!' exclaimed Rebecca. 'I've got a head-ache already. Early bed for me.'

'I'd like to go but I haven't much money,' said Holly.

'Then you keep away,' said the girl. 'The cash just melts in those places.'

Roy and Clive counted over their cash and decided they could spare enough for at least a few rides on the dodgems. After supper they departed on a bus with the sunburnt youth and some other hikers. Rebecca retired to bed, and Holly went back to the paddock to see how the horses were. They were standing dejectedly under a straggling plum-tree, having given up the effort to find any clean grass. Already their sides seemed sunken to Holly. Remembering the thick grass near the hostel she decided to lead them two at a time to feed there. She took Sarah and Ebony first, and their delight at getting some real grass made it worth while. But when the time came to take them back and bring out the other two she could not budge them. Both developed necks of iron, and it looked as if she would have to stay out with them all night until a voice said:

'I say, let me help!'

A girl in baggy jodhpurs, an old raincoat, and hair in plaits came over the road and took Sarah's rope.

'I do know a bit about horses,' she went on, as if apologizing. 'I have a lesson every week at the riding school. Aren't these lovely horses? You're on a riding tour, aren't you?'

'Yes, but how did you know?' asked Holly, welcoming a helper.

'We live down the road where your horses are. You are lucky. I wish I had a horse of my own. I don't mind what I do with them.'

'Well, if you can help me get these two back and bring out the others it would just about save my life!'

With the aid of Barbara, which the girl said was her name,

Sarah and Ebony were inveigled back to the paddock and Alaska and Baynard given their turn on the grass. When Barbara saw Baynard she was overawed by his height, but she thought Alaska was the prettiest of them all which slightly nettled Holly, who thought Ebony surpassed the other three in sheer good looks. But it passed the time away having someone to chat to.

When she got back to the hostel Roy and Clive were still out, although it was close on ten o'clock and shutting-up time.

They'll get into trouble for being late, she thought, remembering reading something in the rules on that subject.

14

'Don't get lost in the mist'

ROY and Clive came down to breakfast the next morning wearing faintly guilty expressions. In answer to Holly's query as to how they had enjoyed themselves Roy said:

'Oh, all right, thanks.'

'What time did you get back?'

'Well, as a matter of fact it was a bit late. After the fun fair we went on to the ice rink, which was jolly fine, but after that we got on the wrong bus, and by the time we got back here the hostel was shut.'

'Then how did you get in?' inquired Rebecca. 'Up a drain pipe?'

'We couldn't find a suitable one so we had to knock up the warden. That didn't make us very popular, and we shall have to pay a fine.'

'But it was worth it,' added Clive. 'The rink was simply marvellous. We hired skates and got on quite decently after a few spills.'

'How much did all that cost?' asked Holly.

'It was cheap really, for what it was, I mean. But it did make a bit of a hole in our cash. In fact I shall have to take some out of my savings bank. What a good thing I didn't lose the book when Alaska ran away in the Forest!'

'I thought you'd come back broke,' said Rebecca. 'And, don't forget, we've got to buy some more oats for the horses this morning – it's a dashed expensive way of feeding them!'

After breakfast there was a race for the brooms and dustpans in order to get through their duties as soon as possible. Roy and

Clive were put on to sweep out their dormitory, and Rebecca and Holly to do the dining-room.

'I do wish people wouldn't spill so many crumbs,' complained Rebecca, clattering chairs from one side of the room to the other.

When they were finished the warden gave them their cards, duly stamped with the name of the hostel, and they were free to go. A thick mist was blotting out the downs beyond the rows of wet red roofs. It was cold and rather depressing. Armed with more packets of oats they went down to the paddock where they found Barbara already at work, and Holly introduced her to the others.

'I borrowed a brush from the school,' she said, 'but I couldn't do much grooming because their coats are so damp.'

'They stink of chicken,' said Clive, wrinkling his nose. 'Alaska's mane is full of manure!'

The oats did not last long. Ebony was so determined to get his share this time that when the bedraggled hens gathered round he drove them fiercely away and pretended to kick the donkey.

'Better saddle up and start off,' said Rebecca. 'And if they dry by midday brush them down then.'

When they went to fetch the saddles and bridles the old man was out, and Rosie refused to let them enter the woodshed. Their coaxing words only increased her fury.

'We shall never get off at this rate,' said Holly, after fruitlessly sacrificing half a sausage-roll which happened to be in her pocket 'I wonder where the old man has got to?'

'I think he does his shopping about now. I'll run and look for him,' offered the obliging Barbara.

At length she returned with the old man, who was carrying a basket of groceries. He seized Rosie's chain, and dragging her into the kitchen slammed the door on her, remarking as he did so :

'Her's a wunnerful watch-dog. Tore the trouser leg right off the electric light man. No business round the back, I told him.'

While they were saddling up Holly asked Roy in a whisper

whether he would let Barbara come a little way with them on Sarah in return for her help.

'Why pick on Sarah?' he asked, feeling a little out of sorts after the previous evening's gaiety.

'Well, she *is* really the best behaved. If you like you can ride Ebony and I'll walk.'

Roy had been wanting to ride Ebony for the last two days, and brightened up immediately. Barbara's eyes sparkled when he told her she could have Sarah for a little way. Meanwhile Rebecca was shouting at the old man to find out how much they owed him for the use of his paddock. After giving the matter deep thought he replied:

'Two bob apiece.'

'I think that's steep!' complained Clive as they rode off. 'His donkey got more of our oats than the horses did of his grass.'

'Well, at least it was somewhere to keep them for the night.'

Although they had liked the hostel they were glad to be leaving Patcham and heading for the open country again. Barbara sat rather stiffly, trying to put all her riding lessons into practice at once, while Sarah paced steadily along quite unaware that she was the object of so much care. Roy, being heavier than Holly and, although stronger, slightly less agile, had some difficulty in mounting Ebony with his rucksack on his back.

'It's like getting on a merry-go-round in motion,' he grunted on at last reaching the saddle.

Holly, pumping along on foot, was glad of the chance to watch Ebony in action, for the glimpse of him crashing through the wood at Arundel was all she had hitherto seen of him under the saddle. She was enthralled by the way in which he carried himself with his neck arched and his long thick tail streaming out, and his rounded hoofs coming down firmly and squarely. His knee action was rather high, but it added to the gaiety of his carriage.

Half a mile of road brought them to the open downs, only the mist made them anything but open just then. They let

Barbara have a little canter on the turf, and then Roy got back on Sarah and Holly mounted Ebony.

'Good-bye, and thank you ever so much for the ride.'

'Good-bye, and thank you for helping.'

'Don't get lost in the mist,' Barbara called after them before running back down the hill.

'It would be funny if we did, wouldn't it?' said Holly.

'I'm going to keep a jolly close watch on the compass,' said Roy. 'I thought of that straight away. Our next hostel is at a place called Jevington, and I've checked up that it's due south-east, so if we keep to that we can't go far wrong.'

'Famous last words,' muttered Rebecca.

They rode for some way without the mist clearing, crossing a main road where the cars had their sidelights on, and mounting again by a bridle-path out of the village of Falmer. The horses snatched at mouthfuls of grass and clover as they moved along with lowered heads. Sometimes it was a job to get them by the succulent tufts.

'You know, the poor things are still hungry,' said Holly. 'Let's stop for a bit and let them have a good tuck in, and perhaps the mist will clear soon.'

So they took off the bridles and the horses fell greedily to work. It was damp and chilly standing about, and the riders stamped their feet and blew on their fingers, for they had no gloves.

'I wish we'd bought some food in the village down there,' said Roy who, in spite of having eaten an excellent breakfast, always felt hungry when there was nothing else to occupy him. 'We won't pass another village until we get to Southease on the river Ouse.'

'How far is that?'

'About five miles over the downs.'

'We shall be easily there by dinner time,' said Rebecca, the only one with a watch. 'Southease sounds a nice comfortable kind of place for a meal.'

By the end of twenty minutes they fancied that the sky looked lighter, so they pushed the bits back into the horses'

reluctant mouths and rode on. The mist began to break, and for
a minute a gleam of pale sun shone waveringly. A bird started
a little song in some low bushes, but stopped again abruptly.
Although the view was still restricted they could now see several
hundred yards ahead, and the horses moved on more keenly.
Ebony began to pull at his bit and swing sideways towards
Alaska, as if inviting her to have a gallop.

'No flying off headlong,' warned Rebecca. 'You don't want
to end up at the bottom of a chalk pit.'

After the last snatch of bird song a deathly quiet came over
the downs. The horses' hoofs passed noiselessly over the damp
turf. It was still as well as silent. No wings flapped in the sky,
no sheep or cattle moved on the visible slopes. There was a
peculiar feeling of desolation which was different from the
ordinary pleasant loneliness of the downs, and Holly noticed
that the others were looking uneasily about them, while Roy
had got out his map and compass. They came upon a number
of tracks radiating off from the well-marked one which they
had been following and which now grew fainter, so that it was
hard to tell which was the main one.

'We should come to a farm at any minute,' said Roy with a
puzzled frown. 'I wonder why there are no animals about?'

'The grass looks as if it hadn't been grazed for years,' said
Rebecca. 'What's that dark thing on the next hillside?'

They pressed on towards a large dark object looming out of
the mist.

'Why, it's an enemy tank, and it's coming our way!' exclaimed Roy.

They stopped in alarm, and the sinister crouching shape
appeared to halt too. They listened for a shout, but none came,
so they rode cautiously on. Drawing nearer to the tank they
found it had not been moving at all, for it was a derelict, tilted
drunkenly in a deep rut and covered with rust. There was something so gruesome about it in the mist that not even the boys
wished to stop and inspect it closer.

'Then all these paths are tank tracks,' said Roy, 'This must
have been a training area during the war.'

'And look, that must be your farm, or what's left of it,' said Clive, pointing to some crumbling mounds of stone and brick. 'They must have used it for target practice.'

The ruins were already overgrown with weeds, and of a clump of trees which must have once shaded the farm all that remained were some shattered stumps. The emptiness of the surrounding downs was now explained.

'Oh, I don't like this place!' exclaimed Holly, thinking how once this had been a home like Haffeneys. 'Let's get on quickly.'

'There should be a footpath from here over the hill,' said Roy.

'If there's been no farm to walk to for years I should think it would have grown out by now,' said Rebecca.

'Then we shall have to just follow the compass.'

Roy put the compass on a level stone, and took the bearing carefully, directing them straight over the steep hill ahead. The horses lurched up in a series of bounds, stumbling now and then among the ant-hills and huge tussocks of coarse grass. They reached the top blowing hard, and Holly noticed a rusty object in the grass.

'That looks like a shell.'

'It's only a shell case; it's not alive,' said Roy. 'I saw another one on the way up.'

'But there might be live ones about too!' exclaimed Rebecca. 'Let's stick to a track in future, whatever the compass says.'

So the next track they came upon they followed for several miles. And then, just as the sun broke through again, they saw a river gleaming among flat green marshes below them.

'It's the Ouse all right,' said Roy. 'The one Lewes is on, of course, not the Yorkshire one.'

'Well, I should hope not!' said Clive.

In what seemed a very short time after thinking they were completely lost they arrived on a road at the tiny village of Southease. The thatched roofs of the houses and the little church with its Norman tower looked delightful until they discovered there was no shop. Not even a loaf of bread could be bought.

'Nearest you'd get anything to eat would be Lewes or New-haven,' said a soldier who was leaning against a wall.

This was indeed a blow, for all the food they possessed was half a pot of marmite which Rebecca had carried in her luggage all the way.

'That's twice we've muffed this dinner business,' she said. 'We shall just have to push on till we do find a shop.'

'That will be at Alfriston, at least another eight miles,' said Roy.

'Oh, well, we shall be there in time for tea.'

The narrow road crossed the Ouse by means of a rather rudimentary wooden bridge over the sides of which the horses looked apprehensively down at the yellowish water. After that it was downland all the way to Firle Beacon, from which, the last remnants of mist having been blown away, they could see right across the Sussex Weald nearly into Kent. Here they dismounted to rest the horses after the long climb and to give them another chance to graze.

'Which direction is home?' asked Clive.

'Yes, which way?'

Roy spread out the map wider, and they each held a corner to prevent the wind blowing it away while he adjusted his precious compass.

'There you are, due north-east.'

They strained their eyes, but were unable to distinguish any landmarks.

'It must be a long way still,' said Holly. 'I do wonder how Kelly's leg is getting on.'

'It's better, and the swelling has gone down,' said Rebecca.

'And you've known it for two days and never said!' exclaimed Holly.

'Well, you were so down on me for telephoning that I thought the less said the better.'

'Did Dad say how the ferrets were?'

'Did he say anything about my daddy and mummy?'

'And if they got the bull home all right?'

The sudden spate of questions helped to break down the

barrier that events at Arundel had raised between them and Rebecca, and the fact that they had all been thinking of home helped to reunite them still more. Rebecca was more than ready to come half-way, for she had no desire to keep herself aloof, and she even made an effort to look upon Ebony with a forgiving eye.

Their talk was interrupted by a hail from behind. For the first time they became aware of two girls sitting in the shelter of a bank with their rucksacks at their sides, who had set out on foot only that morning from Patcham.

'You must have run practically all the way to get here before us,' said Holly.

'Oh, we've cheated. We hitched a furniture van to Lewes, and then a coal lorry to Southease.'

'You see, we've got an excuse really – blistered heels,' said the other, pointing to strips of adhesive plaster showing above their shoes. 'Are you on your way to Jevington too? It's a lovely ride from Alfriston, they say. All round the head of the Long Man?'

'Is that a pub?' asked Roy.

The girls laughed, and one said :

'You wouldn't get a drink out of him. He's terribly old, prehistoric, I suppose, and he's cut in the side of the Wilmington Down. Covers acres, I believe. You'll see him marked on the map.'

'By the way, I suppose you know they don't do meals at the Jevington hostel,' said her companion. 'If you want supper and breakfast you have to take your own things and cook for yourself.'

'Suffering cats, we haven't had any dinner yet!' exclaimed Rebecca, and the boys looked horrified beyond words.

'Well, if you want to get some food in Alfriston you'd better hurry or the shops will be shutting.'

This galvanized them into action. The surprised horses were bridled in haste and the girths pulled up.

'So long! See you at Jevington!' they shouted to the two girls, and trotted as fast as they dare down the hill towards Alfriston.

Baynard disagreed with trotting downhill, and soon they were strung out in a line with Ebony leading, then Alaska close behind, then Sarah going steadily, and Baynard last of all with his ears back. The spire of Alfriston church rising from the trees in the beautiful Cuckmere valley drew them on, and soon they were coming down the last slope among the houses on the outskirts of the little town.

15

The hazards of a hill grazing

THE boys held the horses by the old market cross while the girls hurried from one timber-fronted shop to the next. They bought a tin of soup, some bacon, and some sticky buns and a loaf from the baker, and then in a fit of inspiration Rebecca bought eight fresh herrings and four large grape-fruit. The next problem was how to carry their purchases. Roy managed to get the grape-fruit into his rucksack, and the buns they ate on the spot. The smaller rations went into their pockets, and the loaf was done up in Clive's mackintosh, but everyone avoided the herrings, which were already beginning to leak through their newspaper wrapping. In the end the boys produced some string and tied the parcel to the side dees of Baynard's saddle. Baynard resented the damp and smelly parcel pressing on his ribs, but although he swished his tail he was too much of a gentleman to buck.

'At any rate we shan't starve now,' said Roy with a sigh of relief.

Feeling the better for the buns and the knowledge that their next two meals were assured, they took the road along the Cuckmere valley, where the river passed between cattle-grazed meadows, willow-shaded and guarded by a great bastion of the downs. Soon they crossed the river and the valley, and followed a white track plunging boldly up on to the downs between sprawling thickets of thorn, wayfaring trees, and mountain ash. The first human being they saw was a shepherd leaning on his crook as he scanned the Weald below him, while his two dogs sat upright beside him watching the stocky, short-woolled sheep drinking from a dew-pond. The deep notes of the sheep bells floated across to them, mingled with the high-pitched bleat of lambs.

'How do they manage to have a pond so high up?' asked Clive.

'Something to do with mist condensation,' replied Roy. 'But they had to be specially made. Our Bert pretends to know how it's done, because his grandfather was a shepherd on the downs.'

'What about this Long Man?' asked Holly.

'We should be passing him pretty soon.'

They scanned the sides of the downs, not quite knowing what to look for. Then Clive pointed out some curious white lines.

'Just as if someone had wobbled about all over the place with a plough.'

'Why, that must be him!' exclaimed Rebecca. 'Only we're looking at him from the wrong end. This is his head immediately below us, and his feet go down to the bottom of the valley.'

A plainly marked track brought them down through a long valley into Jevington. The evening sunlight and lengthening shadows slanted across pasture land so thickly covered in buttercups that it seemed barred with blue and gold, and the Frisian cows feeding there were clean and bright as if freshly painted that day. As the riders trotted along there was a yell from Clive who had dropped behind.

'The herrings!'

The sodden paper had at last given way and, the string being insufficient to hold them, a trail of silver fish now lay scattered in the rear. Gathering up eight herrings, still slippery in spite chalk dust and grass blades sticking to them, was a beastly job, and what next to do with them nobody could think at first.

'Chuck 'em away,' said Holly. 'And let the cats of Jevington come out for a feast.'

'Throw away our supper when we've already missed dinner!' exclaimed Roy. 'I know what we can do.'

With the side of his knife he threaded the string through the gills of the herrings, tied them in a bunch, and with a polite bow handed them like a bouquet to Rebecca.

'Now that's the best idea you've had for a long time,' said Rebecca, tying them back on her saddle.

'You only want a beehive to look like the White Knight in *Alice through the looking-glass*,' giggled Holly.

Once in Jevington the search for a field for the horses began. One farmer they asked was quite willing to have the horses, but the only suitable field had a bull turned out on it.

'The horses would be all right,' he said. 'But I don't know how you could get in there to catch them tomorrow. It's up to you if you like to risk it.'

'No bull for me,' said Rebecca without hesitation.

'I dare say you're wise. There is hill grazing adjoining the road along here, but the owner doesn't live in the village. If you like I'll get on to him by phone.'

The kind farmer went inside, and returned a few minutes later nodding his head.

'That'll be all right. It's the third gate along on your right, and there's a dew-pond for water. But you may have a bit of a walk to fetch them in the morning because they'll have some two hundred acres to run over.'

They lost no time in finding the third gate, and the horses, who knew by now when it was time to put up for the night, turned eagerly in and could barely wait to have their bridles removed before beginning to graze.

'Rather a different sized field to the one they had last night,' said Clive.

The 'field' stretched right out of sight over the crest of a down. At the bottom it was sheltered from the roadside by a fringe of trees, but what happened on the other side of the down they all felt too tired just then to investigate.

'Let's look round the fences after supper,' said Rebecca, stretching her aching legs. 'I'm sure they're much too hungry to move far for several hours. I wish Baynard would roll and rub off some of those fish scales.'

'Alaska still smells of chicken,' said Clive.

They gathered up saddles, bridles, and luggage, and began to look for the youth hostel. This was a low stone house perched on a kind of ledge above the valley. The approach was so steep that it was all they could do to lug their belongings up the slippery grass. The warden eyed their paraphernalia with some surprise.

'You can't have that harness in the dormitories. It'll have to go in the bicycle shed.'

The house was very simply built, an outside stair of rough stones leading to the upper storey, and the water supply was drawn from a well by a small bucket on a rope. The boys thought it was fun letting the bucket down with a plop into the black circle of water far below, but the bucket held so little water that they soon got tired of winding it up. The kitchen and dining-room were in a shed farther up the hill, to which the water for cooking and washing up had to be carried. Savoury smells escaped from the door as the four newcomers approached, and inside they found three burly cyclists in striped socks and knitted caps frying themselves a large panful of sausages and potatoes.

'Come on, bring in your vittles,' said the head cook of the three, waving a fork. 'There are two more gas-rings and the second-best frying-pan's going. Where have you come from today?'

'Patcham.'

'Ah, Brighton, the queen of the south coast! That's where we're off tomorrow. Are you biking, hiking, or hitching?'

'None of those.'

'You can't possibly be canoeing. I just refuse to believe it.'

'No, we're riding.'

'Horseback-riding! Well, I'll be ... It must be the craze round these parts. We've seen several lots of people on horse-back, haven't we, Jock?'

'I think I rather fancy meself on a horse,' said the one called Jock. 'Save all that pedal work uphill.'

'I'll come with you tandem,' said the third youth. 'What about you, Cookie?'

'Me? You won't catch me near a horse, unless they can breed one with rubber hoofs and no teeth.'

This conversation was interrupted by the arrival of the two girls from Firle Beacon. They flung themselves on some benches in exhausted attitudes.

'That climb up here from the road is the last straw on the camel's back,' declared the plumper of the two. 'So you've got here all right. What did you do with your horses?'

'Oh, they're all provided for and stuffing hard,' said Roy. 'What about that supper there's been so much talk about?'

'I think we'd better eat the herrings at once,' said Rebecca. 'They won't keep much longer after being thawed out by Baynard's sweat. There's an awful lot of chestnut hairs as well as other things sticking to them. I wonder if they're really fit to eat?'

But the other three all pointed out that any germs would be killed in the cooking, and soon the smell of frying fish mingled with that of sausages, and the soup and coffee concocted by the two girls. It was a lively meal they all ate together at the long table. The cyclists described their journey down the east coast, and talked of getting to Cornwall by the end of the week. It appeared that two of them shared a tandem while the third went solo. The girls were typists and on their way back to London. They confessed that they relied a great deal on hitching.

'The trouble is we're not fit enough to suddenly start walking twenty or thirty miles a day,' said the plump one. 'Hence our blisters. So now we only walk the very nicest parts, and thumb the rest of the way.'

'Does horse-riding make you stiff?' the other asked Holly.

'Well, no, because we do it at home. But we've had quite a lot of adventures with them. Clive nearly lost his in the New Forest. She got loose with a lot of wild ones.'

'I say, you'd better avoid the New Forest, Cookie,' said Jock. 'They've wild horses there. You wouldn't be safe anywhere.'

Just then two more people came in, a young man and his wife, both wearing untidy, picturesque garments.

'All right, thanks, we've had our supper,' said the man as the others made to move up. 'We only want to make some cocoa. Come along to our tent when you've finished and we'll have a sing-song.'

'He plays in a dance band,' one of the cyclists explained. 'They've got a tent a bit farther up the hill; this hostel has a camping ground too.'

So after everything was washed up they all climbed up to the site of a tiny ridge tent from which the young man produced a disproportionately large accordion – 'squeeze-box', as he called it. There was no camp fire, but they sat in a circle, covering their legs with the blankets from the tent, and sang songs to the accordion until twilight began to well up in the valley below.

'It'll soon be dark,' said Rebecca, during a pause. 'We ought to look at the horses and see if that fence is all right before we turn in.'

They woke Roy who, the least musically inclined, had fallen asleep among the blankets, and bidding the others 'good night' descended rather stiffly to the road. The crests of the downs were blank shapes against a sky of clear greenish blue in which the stars were appearing with a twinkle more silver than gold. The dew was rising and the scent of thyme and sweetbrier filled the damp air. They trudged a long way looking for the horses among the gathering shadows. Some sheep scampered away, and a rabbit thumped its hind legs.

'They must have gone right over the top,' said Holly.

By the time they reached the top of the down it was too dark to distinguish much, and they nearly slipped down the sloping side of the half-empty dew-pond. Right to the south the lights of Eastbourne made a great sparkling patch in the darkness. From across the dene came faintly the notes of the accordion and a single voice singing a plantation song. No horses were visible, and the calling of their names produced no answering whickers.

'We'd better divide and follow the fence round,' said Roy. 'Thre's still just enough light to see if there are any gaps.'

So the boys went to the right and the girls to the left. Stumbling down the hillside the latter found it quite difficult to see the wires between the posts of the fence. Suddenly Holly, who was a little in advance, found herself stepping into space. She drew back too late, and went slipping down, clutching at tufts of grass, until some branches checked her fall a little. With a loud crackling and snapping of twigs she came to rest against the boles of some small trees. Rebecca's voice came echoing after her.

'Holly, Holly, where are you? Are you hurt?'

'I'm all right!' she shouted back. 'You'd better look out for yourself. It's a quarry or something. I'm going to see if I can get out along the bottom.'

'Do you think the horses have fallen over there too?'

This question shouted down by Rebecca made Holly suddenly feel sick. She forced her way through the trees and bushes, nervously imagining each really dark patch to be the prostrate body of a horse. Then she came upon a little track, and the next thing she saw was a light passing swiftly ahead. It was gone like a will-o'-the-wisp before she could call out. Then came a startled snort, and a number of large bodies, one light coloured and one with patches of white, scattered into the darkness with thudding noises. Evidently the horses were all down in the quarry too, apparently uninjured. While Holly was trying to pierce the darkness into which they had vanished she came up against a gate, and then a great beam of light lit it up, and she found to her astonishment that she was standing beside the road and the lights had belonged to passing cars and lorries. Behind her was an open strip of grass, where the horses had been feeding, and a path leading round the bottom of the quarry. She had time to see all this before the car passed. Groping her way up the track she nearly ran into Rebecca and the boys coming down it.

'It's all right. We've met the horses, and they've galloped up on to the hillside again. The fence is quite sound. Where does this track lead?'

'Back on to the road. You don't seem to grasp that I've just plunged over the side of a chalk pit.'

'You said you were all right when I asked,' replied Rebecca. 'The horses had more sense than you and came down by the track.'

'Well, it's lucky you did fall over,' said Roy. 'Otherwise we might have looked for them all night without hitting upon this place. Listen to that!'

The accordion had stopped playing, and among the bushes through which Holly had only recently pushed her way a nightingale began to sing, crooning low at first, then throwing his rounded notes higher and higher towards the crests of the downs.

'That's the first we've heard.' And suppressing further argument they went soft-footed back to the hostel, followed all the way by the nightingale's song.

16

Sarah in a fix

'WE'VE got to make a pretty big decision before we start out today,' said Roy, scrunching his fried bread and taking a swig from the concoction of marmite and hot water which was their substitute for tea. 'There are no hostels directly between us and home, and the distance is too far to ride in one day.'

'Well, that's easy to decide,' said Rebecca. 'We shall have to stay the night at an inn or some kind of bed-and-breakfast place.'

The other three looked uncomfortable, and Holly, with elaborate casualness, conjectured :

'I wonder how much the inns between here and home charge for supper, bed, and breakfast?'

'I don't know about your finances, Rebecca,' said Roy, 'but since paying for our last lot of grub and night's lodgings I'm down to exactly one and three ha'pence.'

'I've only got two and fourpence left,' said Clive. 'When I went to the post office at Patcham they told me I only had five shillings in my saving book, and I couldn't take the whole lot out.'

'I've got two and ten,' said Holly.

'What on earth's made you all so hard up? I've got about fifteen bob, but I'm afraid that won't be enough for us all.'

'We've had unexpected extras to pay for,' said Holly. 'There was my martingale, and the boys had to pay for their skates and dodgems.'

'Those weren't necessities.'

'Well, then there were all those postcards. They come to about tenpence each if you count the stamp. That jolly soon adds up, and we were much too generous at the start.'

'Then there's nothing for it but to fix on where we'll get to by late afternoon and wire home for some money to be sent to the post office,' said Rebecca.

'Oh, no, we can't do that!'

'That would spoil the whole thing if we had to send for money for the last night. They'd all say at home they knew we wouldn't be able to manage properly on what we said.'

'We've got enough money for food,' said Holly. 'Let's have a night out!'

'Out? What do you mean by "out"?' asked Rebecca.

'Sleeping out,' said Clive. 'It would be fun. Do let's.'

'But we haven't a tent or any blankets. It would be much too cold and damp at this time of the year.'

'I bet we could find a barn or a haystack where we could get under the hay,' said Roy. 'It's the only answer. We might have done it earlier and saved more money.'

'And end up by getting rotten colds or rheumatic fever.'

'Oh, come off it, nursy! Your mind runs on horrid diseases. We're not hothouse plants.'

'You can stay in an hotel if you like,' said Roy, 'I'm going to sleep out.'

'And me!'

'Me too!'

'You're making it jolly awkward for me as usual,' said Rebecca.

'We told you before you were only the figurehead,' said Roy. 'And the figurehead has to go with the ship, you know.'

'If you really feel you must look after our healths you'd better come and sleep out with us and see that we keep our feet out of the dew,' added Clive.

'Yes, come on, Rebecca,' said Holly, 'we'd much rather you were with us because you're so good at arranging things.'

She was anxious to avoid another disagreement with her cousin so near the end of their travels.

'Well, you don't suppose I should go and stay in an hotel while you three are sleeping under a hedge, do you? But I do at least insist on a barn or a roof of some kind. Have you looked up a route, Roy?'

'Yes, we leave the downs pretty soon and there should be a bridle-path right across Pevensey Levels to the Weald, and after that it's mostly lanes until we get to the Rother marshes, but I shouldn't think we'd manage that before tonight.'

'We shan't get anywhere if we sit on here,' said Holly, jumping up and beginning to collect the plates.

After they had washed up and folded their blankets, and said various farewells, they collected their saddlery and staggered down the steep slope with it.

'It's quite sad to think that this is our last hostel,' said Holly, looking back at the little stone house above them.

'They've been jolly useful to us,' acknowledged Rebecca. 'And although I've never remained so grubby for so long we could hardly have managed this trip without them.'

When they got to the field, expecting to have a long trudge after the horses, as the farmer had warned, they found them quite near the gate. But this advantage was spoilt by Sarah, who was in an unusually crotchety mood and refused to be caught. She did not run away, but kept just out of Roy's reach in a particularly annoying manner. One by one they all tried to catch her without success.

'It's the downland air gone to her head,' said Holly.

'It's just sheer cussedness,' retorted Roy. 'Do you remember she was like this once when we were going to a gymkhana and made us miss the first events?'

The other three horses were brushed, saddled, and bridled, and still Sarah roamed at large. Roy grew more and more hot trudging after her, while she swished her tail, nibbled grass, and neatly evaded him. At last he said :

'You'd better take the others into the road. She may change her mind if she thinks she's being left behind.'

When Sarah saw the others leaving her she became agitated and cantered to and fro neighing. Finding the gate shut in her face she charged at it, and at the last second attempted to jump. Being much too close to take off properly, her forelegs went over while her hind ones remained behind, leaving her stuck half-way across the gate.

'Hold her head!' shouted Roy from the rear.

Pulling Baynard after her Rebecca ran and seized Sarah's halter to prevent her from struggling. But Sarah's natural good sense prevailed at last. Finding after one heave that she was quite unable to get herself free, she made no more attempts, and with a touching faith in her human companions remained straddled across the gate waiting for them to get her off. Their first action, after tying up the horses, was a concerted attempt to lift the gate off its hinges. But with Sarah's weight pressing down on the top bar this was impossible.

'We shall either have to get a saw or some men,' said Rebecca, raising a heated face.

'We shall have to pay for the gate if we saw it up,' said Clive.

'Well, we can't just leave her there, you idiot,' retorted Roy. 'We must get her off quickly before she injures something inside.'

'I'll run to the farm while you're arguing,' cried Holly, and set off at top speed.

Opposite the hostel she saw the three cyclists with striped socks getting their machines down the steep bank.

They're as hefty as any farm men! she thought, and gave them a hail: 'Come at once! We're in an awful fix.'

They abandoned their bicycles immediately.

'What's the matter? What's gone wrong?'

Holly explained jerkily, beseeching them to hurry, and they were not long in arriving at the scene of the disaster. It was a very odd scene to come upon with Sarah's brown-and-white face gazing anxiously out from the group of equally anxious people gathered before the gate.

'Well, I'd never believe it! I thought this only happened in funny pictures!' exclaimed Jock.

'Believe it or not, old man, we shall have to do something. And before we can get that gate off its hinges we shall have to de-rust them.'

Cookie ran back to his bicycle and returned with a tool bag. They lost no time in getting to work on the hinges with an oil-can and tyre-levers. While this was going on a roadman with his hand-cart arrived on the scene.

'God bless my soul!' he exclaimed with some justification.

'Hi, old chap, lend us your shovel!' cried Jock. 'And we shall want the use of your shoulder too in half a second.'

With the sharp edge of the shovel they quickly finished free-ing the hinges. Then telling the girls to hold on to Sarah's head the six strong men and true put their shoulders to the hinge end of the gate. Poor Sarah grunted with discomfort as the gate was slowly levered upwards and the top bar dug far-ther into her stomach, but she was by now too winded to struggle if she wanted to. Red in the face and with the veins standing out in their necks, the men and boys toiled and strained until at last with a shout of triumph the gate slipped off its hinges and dropped to ground level.

'Tilt it a mort, and then slip it out sideways, or she'll get her legs between the bars,' advised the roadman.

This was easy, for although relieved from the pressure Sarah still stood as if paralysed with her legs straddled. Fearing that she might be internally injured they held on to her, making soothing noises, while Roy felt gently underneath. Then, as if coming out of a trance, she brought her legs together, shook herself, and, walking briskly over to her companions, began to graze.

'I don't believe she's any the worse for all that!' said Holly.

'That's a good strong bit of timber to have stood the strain,' said the roadman, admiringly looking at the gate which two of the cyclists were replacing.

'It's a good strong horse too,' said Rebecca. 'I wonder she didn't break her ribs.'

'Well, thanks tremendously, all of you,' said Roy. 'I don't know what we should have done if you hadn't come.'

'Don't mentch,' replied Cookie. 'Next time I meet a horse I can look it in the eye now I've done something for one of its relations.'

The cyclists went back to their machines and the roadman to his hand-cart, and, deciding after further examination that Sarah really was none the worse for her misadventure, Roy saddled up.

'But I shall lead her for a bit, just in case she feels sore. We've got to keep to the road anyhow for the next few miles.'

Discussing the past event, and how very differently it might have ended, they travelled along the lane past Wannock and out on to the main road among the rows of modern houses surrounding Polegate. They were not long in finding another by-way leading on to Pevensey Levels.

'Better look your last on the downs,' said Roy.

Although they had not yet come far inland a light mist hung between them and the downs. The great chalk hills had withdrawn behind this veil and looked so remote that it was hard to believe only a short time before they had cantered along the airy crests and looked down upon the levels as somewhere far away.

'We have ridden through some different sorts of country in the last few days,' remarked Rebecca. 'The Forest and industrial areas, the Hampshire downs and the South Downs, and now Pevensey Levels.'

'And the Hampshire downs weren't at all the same as the south downs, just as these levels look quite different from Romney Marsh,' added Holly.

As Sarah was walking briskly along with no sign of stiffness Roy mounted her. Shortly after this they hit the bridle-path he had looked out on the map running across the two levels of Down and Horse Eye. The path had broad strips of grass between the wheel tracks, and it twisted so frenziedly to avoid the dikes that, as they cantered in single file, they were frequently all facing different directions. The grass was much more bright and lush than on the downs and grazed by herds of dark red Sussex cattle with wide white horns tipped with black. The sheep they saw made home seem quite near, for they were of the big Romney Marsh breed.

The miles of level turf stretching before them was a great

strain upon the eager natures of Ebony and Alaska. At first their riders managed to keep them back, cantering decorously with Sarah and Baynard along the curving track. But they fretted and pulled until at last they were given their heads and allowed to gallop on.

'We shall only numb their mouths if we keep tugging at them!' Holly shouted to Clive, who nodded in agreement.

Baynard and Sarah were anxious to keep their end up too, but their riders held them in, thinking that it would give the other two more chance to pull up when the time came. Holly was enjoying the gallop. She felt she could still stop Ebony if necessary, and so long as she kept to the track there could be no danger. The light wind whistled past her ears and the black mane flapped against her hands as Ebony stretched out into a long rhythmical stride. Suddenly the track took a much sharper turn than before. A warning shout from Clive came simultaneously with the shine of water just ahead. There was a perceptible halt in Ebony's stride as he too saw the dike ahead, and for an instant Holly actually felt herself going on alone. It was only an instant, for Ebony gathered himself together in time to clear the dike, landing on the far side with a grunt as Holly pitched half-way up his neck.

By the time she had got back into the saddle, found both stirrups, and pulled Ebony up by the aid of circling, the others were crossing the dike by a low, parapetless bridge, which the track had swerved so violently to join.

'Did you mean to jump that?' asked Roy,

'Of course not. I didn't know the beastly thing was there until too late.'

'I went into it as near as ninepence,' said Clive. 'Alaska just managed to get round the bend with me clinging on by my eyelids.'

'I told you that animal would land you in a jam one day, Holly,' said Rebecca.

'But he didn't land me in it – he cleared it beautifully in spite of my being half-way up his neck. If he had stopped I'd have landed right in the middle of the dike.'

'He certainly spread himself smashingly,' said Roy. 'It looked as if he landed with feet to spare.'

Holly glowed with pleasure.

'Oh, I do hope daddy lets me keep him,' she burst out involuntarily.

'Well, it's only just over one more day before you know the worst,' said Clive, meaning to be encouraging.

'Better look out that Ebony doesn't charge straight at the canal when you get home,' said Rebecca. 'He won't clear that in a hurry!'

The wooded hills of the Sussex Weald now loomed ahead, and before long they had left the levels and were clopping along the winding lane by Hurstmonceaux. A great rosy-red building with towers, turrets, and battlements stood beyond the horse-chestnuts.

'Why, it's a castle!' said Holly.

'You can't have a brick castle,' objected Clive.

'It is one just the same.'

'I bet it wouldn't stand up to much bombarding.'

'I think it's the best castle I've seen yet,' said Rebecca. 'Nothing damp or grey or ruinous; it quite reconciles me to ancient monuments.'

As they left the castle behind they met a boy scuffling along with his hands in his pocket, obviously bored and needing a diversion.

'Hallo!' he greeted them, brightening. 'Heard the Ghostly Drummer today?'

'What Ghostly Drummer?' asked Clive, his eyes bulging.

'Him that haunts the castle. They say there's a chest there he's guarded for years and years. I bet you wouldn't go in there at night.'

'How much do you bet?' asked Roy, thinking that this might be a good way of restoring his finances.

'It's no good saying, 'cos you wouldn't be allowed in.'

'Come on, he's only pulling your leg,' said Rebecca.

But Holly, liking the idea of the ghost, lingered behind.

'What's in the chest?' she asked the boy.

'I'll tell you a secret – there never was any chest. The Drummer was one of a gang of smugglers pretending to be a ghost to frighten people away. But don't breathe a word – promise?'

'Of course, but why mustn't I?'

'One day I might want to do some smuggling myself.'

When Holly caught the others up again she found them discussing the important subject of food.

'Let's get it while we're near a village,' Roy was saying. 'For all we know it may be early closing day.'

'Don't let's buy any more fish, unless it's in a tin,' said Rebecca.

'We'd better not buy anything that needs cooking in case we can't have a fire.'

It was rather tiresome having to burden themselves with parcels and bread so soon, but they agreed it was the wisest plan, and laid out their few shillings to their best advantage at the village stores. Then they rode on through the tangle of narrow lanes with high sprawling hedges which went burrowing through the Sussex Weald. This land, which from the top of Firle Beacon had looked nearly flat, they now discovered was honeycombed by streams running through steep and winding valleys. The lanes switched merrily up and down from one valley to the next between woods and small irregularly shaped fields, and farms that were dotted almost within hailing distance of one another.

By late afternoon they had reached the crest of the long hill near Brightling from where, looking northwards into the blue distance, they could actually see into Kent. When Roy told them this Holly felt a strange thrill – strange because it meant that the end of their journey was near, and she had enjoyed almost every minute of it. But there was little time to dwell on the paradox, for Rebecca said:

'We'd better soon start looking for somewhere to sleep.'

'But it won't be dark yet,' said Clive.

'I know, but we may not be lucky straight away, and we don't want to get benighted without any cash.'

With evening falling and the air growing a little chill the prospect of sleeping out was not quite so inviting. A roof of some sort was essential, and now that they had left it too late to send for money they realized that they had thrown themselves entirely on the hospitality of the countryside.

17

Beggars on horseback

As farms were the most likely places to give them a night's lodging they decided to try their luck in pairs. Leaving their ponies with the girls, Roy and Clive with an air of great resolution strode into the next farm they came to. They soon returned, shaking their heads and looked rather red in the face.

'The old geezer there wouldn't take us seriously,' complained Roy. 'I don't know who he really thought we were, but he said he didn't want any diddicoys or gipsies hanging round his place and we'd better clear off sharp.'

'He probably did mistake you for diddicoys – you look dirty and untidy enough,' said Rebecca.

'Can't be much worse than you two.'

'That's a fact. You and I, Holly, had better tidy up a bit before we try.'

So when they came to another farm the girls dragged a comb painfully through their tangled locks, rubbed their faces with their least dirty handkerchiefs, and tried to smooth out their crumpled collars. Even these efforts did not make them look exactly spick and span, and as they walked up the garden path to the house Holly grew more and more conscious of the two ragged holes Ebony's brisk action had worn in her jodhpurs and through which her bare legs showed. The garden was unusually trim for one belonging to a farm, and the smart lady who answered their tap on the polished brass knocker looked at her callers with distaste.

'The farm's nothing to do with me,' she answered their timid request. 'I only rent the house.'

'Could you tell us where the farmer lives, please?'

'Oh, he doesn't live in this village. You could try the

foreman. I believe he lives somewhere down there,' pointing along the road they had come. 'You'd better ask in the village. Good evening.'

When they came back and reported this conversation Roy said:

'I don't suppose the foreman would give us permission off his own bat. We'd better push on again.'

'Third time lucky,' said Rebecca.

The horses, having made up their minds to spend the night at this farm, were distinctly annoyed at having to go on again. With difficulty they were urged away from the farm entrance, and mooched along the road snatching at sprays in the hedges to show how hungry they were.

'We're just as hungry as you are!' exclaimed Holly, hauling at Ebony, whose neck muscles were like bands of iron when it came to stretching out for food. 'But we can't stop till we've found somewhere for the night.'

The road now ran through a wooded countryside where there were a few houses but no farms. Evening was well advanced; the sun had slipped behind the tree-tops, and swifts were streaking to and fro across the greenish sky shrieking their warning of nightfall. The rattle of a lawn-mower in one of the gardens and the strains of a familiar wireless programme issuing from an open window brought the homelessness of their plight more keenly than ever before the travellers. They could not ride all night, and the possibility of having to sit by the road-side holding the horses until daybreak loomed bleakly before them. With noble self-restraint Rebecca refrained from making any allusions to her doubts about their plan that morning.

'I wonder if we went to a police station whether they would lend us some money,' said Roy at last.

'They might put us in the lock-up, but I don't know how they'd manage about the horses,' said Rebecca.

'This looks like a turning down to a farm,' said Holly.

When the farm came in sight they could not agree upon who should put their request. While they were arguing two girls ran out of one of the buildings.

'I say, look who's come to visit us, Rosamund. What a lovely lot of horses. Look at the skewbald one! Where are you going so late in the evening?'

'We're trying to find somewhere to stay for the night,' said Holly.

'What, a hotel?'

'No, a field for the horses and a barn for us.'

'We haven't any money, you see,' said Clive.

'And we're on a riding tour.'

'Well, you must stay here, of course,' said the younger of the two who, by their equal fairness and lanky build, were obviously sisters.

'Yes, we're mad about horses, and we'd love you to stay for a week. The horses could go in the orchard, couldn't they, Jane, and they could sleep in the straw house?'

'Not in the orchard, Rosamund, not with Simon – there might be a fight. But they could easily go in the field beyond. And you could have our tent if you'd rather sleep out there with them. We're not allowed to camp out until the summer holidays.'

'It's a bit chilly. I think the straw house sounds warmer,' said Rebecca.

'Yes, it's lovely and cosy in there,' said Rosamund. 'There are rather a lot of cats, but they're awfully nice ones.'

'But what about your parents? Hadn't we better ask them first if we can stop?'

A look of meaning passed between the two sisters, then Jane, the elder, said:

'Well, you see, daddy's out at the moment. He's gone to London, and he won't be back till after dark, so he won't really know you're here till the morning, which won't matter much, 'cos you'll be practically gone by then, I suppose.'

'But surely you're not all alone here?'

'Oh, no, there's mummy. She's in bed with a rotten cold and a head, and doesn't want to be bothered again tonight. That only leaves Grace who does for us, and she's slipped down to the village for half an hour. Oh, you must stay. We'll be terribly disappointed if you don't. Nothing nice like this has happened for a whole week.'

'We shall have to think about it first,' said Rebecca, motioning the others aside. 'We can hardly stay here without their father's permission. It might turn out to be most awkward if he came home and didn't want us here.'

'He could only tell us to do a bunk,' said Roy.

'Let's risk it and stay here,' begged Clive. 'My back's aching like it did before. I can't ride another step. And, anyhow, Alaska and Ebony have made up their minds to stay. I'm sure we couldn't budge them tonight.'

'That's quite true. It would be an awful job to drag Ebony back on to the road again,' said Holly.

'Oh, yes, you're just going to stay,' chimed in the sisters, and Jane added:

'They've left the corn bin unlocked, so we can give your horses lots of oats.'

It was the mention of the oats that turnèd the scale. None of the horses were so fat as when they started out; Baynard showed it in particular, his large frame being the least adapted to grubbing a living nomad fashion. A feed of corn would go a long way towards putting new life into them and counteracting the effects of this long day on the road.

'All right then. Only let's hope your father comes back from London in a good mood.'

'He hardly ever does,' said Rosamund cheerfully.

With whoops of glee the sisters showed them the way to the stables, and helped to unsaddle the horses.

'You can put all the tack in the harness-room,' said Jane, and she and Rosamund ran to and fro with it themselves, and then dragging in buckets of oats which they tipped lavishly into the mangers.

'Steady on, not too many!' exclaimed Rebecca, as the horses with eyes gleaming plunged their noses into the feast. 'They're not used to corn, and it might make them ill if they gorge.'

It was dusk by the time the horses had finished, and almost dark in the stables.

'We have electric light, you know, but we'd better not switch it on in case Grace sees it and starts asking questions.

We'll show you the way to the field now. Can I lead Alaska?'
'And me Sarah?'

A track round the side of the orchard led to the field below
it, which was on the sloping side of the valley and hidden from
the farm by the fruit-trees. As they went down it in single file
there was a neighing in the orchard, and a fat figure with a
white blaze careered about under the dark trees.

'That's Simon,' said Jane. 'He's most frightfully intelligent,
and shakes hands, but he has got rather a loud voice.'

Quite ignoring Simon's shrieks the horses lay down and
rolled directly they were turned loose, and then began to graze
as if the feed of a few minutes before had never existed.

'I hope Simon shuts up before daddy comes back or he'll be
suspicious,' said Rosamund.

The visitors agreed fervently.

'What about supper? Have you got any food?' asked Jane.
'We'd ask you to share ours but Grace may be back at any
minute now. We could get you something from the larder
though.'

'Oh, we've got our own food,' said Rebecca hastily, for her
conscience was pricking her over the oats.

'But I would like a drink,' said Roy longingly.

'We can bring you some milk. Get the big jug from the
larder, Rosamund, and some cups, and I'll bring the rugs from
the hall.'

The two little girls sped away to the house and soon returned
laden.

'There's no light in the straw house, so we've brought you
a torch. We'll see you in and then we must fly. Grace just came
in at the back door as we came out of the front.'

The straw house, so far as they could make out, was a little
lodge adjoining the stable, windowless, and half filled with
trusses. As they opened the door there was a rustle in the straw
and some small animals shot out through a gap in the boarding.

'Only the cats. One of them has kittens. Be careful not to lie
on them; they're in that corner.' Jane directed the light to
where some faint mewing came from behind a truss. 'Good

night. Sleep tight. We'll be along as early as we can to see you.'

'You'd better keep as quiet as mice when daddy comes back,' added Rosamund. 'Just in case, you know.'

With this not very reassuring parting remark the sisters trotted off back to the house, and the travellers sat down in the straw and unpacked their provisions.

'Well, it's certainly cosy in here,' said Holly, working herself between some trusses. 'We ought to sleep all right.'

'Lucky the straw's trussed and not baled,' said Roy. 'That wouldn't be very comfortable to lie on!'

'I wonder what the farmer will say tomorrow,' said Clive, now beginning to get a little nervous.

'Time enough to worry tomorrow. At least we shall have had our night's lodgings. Shall I hack up the loaf?'

It was the strangest meal they had ever shared, sitting among the trusses with the stiff beam of the torch now shining on the dusty boarding, now on a grubby hand holding a cup of milk. They ate and drank greedily, and all the milk, the whole of the loaf with butter, cheese, buns, and a tin of pilchards in tomato sauce soon disappeared.

'What shall we do for breakfast?' asked Holly, feeling through the empty bags.

'We shall have to buy something in the first village we come to,' said Rebecca.

The other three did not like to remind her that their last coppers had gone on the food now consumed. Unless Rebecca offered to treat them it looked as though they had had their last meal until they reached home.

They shared out the rugs, wrapped themselves up, turned off the torch, and worked themselves deeper into the straw, glad to be able to stretch out their tired legs, cramped with riding so far that day. Holly was shaken out of the doze into which she had soon slipped by a violent disturbance just in her ear.

'What is it? What's that!'

'Cats!' came Roy's disgusted voice. 'They were after the pilchard tin, but they've bolted now.'

The kittens in the corner were mewing loudly, and for a time sleep evaded them. The straw rustled as they turned over. An animal, horse or cow, bumped about in the next building, and then some owls started an argument overhead. Roy crawled to the door to drive them away, and the hooting broke off abruptly, but the tang of the night air and smell of dew blew in on their faces.

'Shut the door! You're letting in the damp!'

They had just got comfortable again, and the kittens had gone to sleep, when the pony in the orchard began to neigh again. This time the horses answered him, and then there was the rumble of hoofs along the valley and a fresh burst of neighing.

'That last lot sounds like cart-horses,' muttered Roy.

'The whole valley seems full of horses by the row,' said Rebecca.

Just then they heard the swish of wheels coming down the lane. As the car rounded the last bend its headlights stabbed through the cracks between the boarding and for a second lit their tense faces. It pulled up with a creak in the garage close to the house and the door slammed. Guessing it to be the farmer returning they all four froze in the straw like rabbits sensing the presence of a stoat. There was the sound of the garage doors being dragged to and the click of a lock. The horses, who had quietened at the approach of the car, now began neighing again, and the rumble of hoofs sounded much nearer, punctuated by snorts and sharp squeals.

The farmer, instead of going into the house, came rapidly into the yard. As he passed the straw house they heard him mutter:

'. . . better find out what's upset them, I . . .'

He went into the harness-room, and switched on the light on the other side of the thin boarding.

'He'll see our saddles!' whispered Clive, and another startled exclamation confirmed this.

The farmer did not stay there long, but strode rapidly back across the yard and into the house. As he opened the door they heard him shout:

'Grace, Grace, what's been going on?'

'The fat's in the fire now,' said Rebecca. 'We shall have to come out of hiding. It'll be a pretty fix if we're turned out on the road at this time of night!'

'But what can be making the horses gallop about and squeal like that?' asked Holly.

'Yes, I think we ought to go down and see what's happening to them,' said Roy. 'They may run into some wire in the dark. Where's the torch?'

'Well, if the farmer orders us off, I don't know how we're going to catch them tonight,' remarked Clive.

By the time they had found the torch, unwrapped themselves from the rugs, and stumbled out into the cold night air the quiet house opposite had been stirred to life by the shouts for Grace. Lights flicked up in most of the windows, and a babel of voices floated through the open door where a broad-shouldered figure was silhouetted against the light.

'Well, why on earth didn't you make sure the field was safe before you put them in there?' asked a man's voice crossly.

He was answered by a confusion of replies in which a shriller voice said something about a jug of milk.

'Come on; we've got to face the music,' said Rebecca.

She led the way across the yard, followed by a somewhat irresolute band.

'It's us,' she said, as they came into the light from the door. 'They're our horses making the noise, and we're to blame for everything.'

'Good heavens, what a crew!' exclaimed the farmer. 'Why, you're all of you mostly kids. What are you doing here on your own at this time of night with all these horses? You look as if you'd run away from a home.'

There was justice for his last remark, for the shaft of light revealed not only their normal untidiness, but the bits of straw clinging to their clothing and hair, and the somewhat scared expressions of their faces. Before anyone could reply Jane broke out:

'But we've told you, daddy, they're on a riding tour and had nowhere else to stay. They just had to stay here.'

'We never thought about the gate between the fields being open,' added Rosamund.

The sisters were in pyjamas with coats pulled hastily on top. Behind them loomed a broad-bosomed figure with grey hair straggling down on a white lace collar. This must be Grace, who added pityingly:

'Well, all I can say is they look as if they needed that milk, the poor things!'

'What a party to come home to!' exclaimed the farmer. 'Where are my boots? Your horses have got mixed up with my cart-horses, and if we don't get down there and separate them quick they may do some damage.'

Rosamund dragged out a large pair of rubber boots.

'Can we come?' she cried.

'Yes, I suppose you'd better.'

'Put your slacks on and your riding coats,' commanded Grace. 'You'll be catching your deaths in this night air and dew.'

'Here, take a torch and run to the harness-room and get my horses' halters,' said the farmer to Roy, and sat down on a chair in the passage to drag his boots on.

'We're awfully sorry, we are really,' began Holly, but he waved aside her apologies.

'We'll go into that later. The thing to do first is to sort these horses out. I hope you can catch yours. One of mine is only a colt.'

The boys returned with three hemp halters and the two little girls clattered downstairs again with more clothes on. They had three torches among them, but this did not save them from stumbling into the ruts as they all hurried down the track to the field. For a moment it was quiet in the valley.

'The trouble is there are three fields opening into each other,' said the farmer. 'It won't be too easy to spot them if they keep quiet.'

He had hardly spoken when there was a high squeal and a drumming of hoofs close at hand. In the starlight they could just make out what appeared to be a huge herd of horses stampeding past the gate.

'I can see Alaska!' cried Clive.

They turned on all the torches and swept the field. The horses, hearing their voices, had drawn up in a semicircle, and the light glinted on their eyeballs and the white parts of their coats.

The riders began to call their horses' names as enticingly as they could:

'Sarah! Baynard! Ebo! 'Laska!'

The two little girls chimed in with the names of the cart-horses: 'Bob! Duchess! Blossom, darling!' But taking care to keep behind their father, for the cart-horses loomed immense against the night.

Just as it seemed as if they were going to catch the horses without difficulty the cart-horse colt reared playfully up and nearly came down on Alaska's back. She flung up her heels with a squeal, and this upset the whole party. They wheeled about and galloped off into the night, the sound of their hoofs growing fainter and fainter.

'Sounds as if they've gone right down to the bottom,' said the farmer in the resigned tones of one who has spent a lifetime dealing with animals. 'The best thing we can do is to shut them in the bottom field before we try to catch any of them. It's only four acres so they can't get far from us.'

It was a long trudge down through the dew-drenched grass among tussocks, rabbit holes, and mole hills until they located the horses again in the small field. Here they managed to catch Sarah, Baynard, and Alaska, who fortunately had their halters on, while the farmer got the two older cart-horses. The colt ran round bucking and kicking, but of Ebony there was no sign. Holly called and called without getting any reply.

'Haven't you got them all?' asked the farmer.

'No, Ebony's missing. Oh, where can he be?'

'Better get yours into the next field and the gate up, and then we'll have a look for him.'

Jane and Rosamund bravely held on to the cart-horses, with

whom they seemed to be on intimate terms, while their father held the colt at bay and the others were able to get the three riding horses through the gate.

'Better take them right up to the top field,' he directed them, 'and shut them in there. With a whole field between perhaps they'll settle down and give us some peace for the rest of the night.'

'But I must find Ebony. I'm sure something awful's happened to him,' said Holly in tragic tones.

When they had shut the horses safely in the top field they all joined in the search for Ebony. The torch-light revealed a great many weals scooped in the turf by the galloping hoofs, and an old water tank, which for a moment they mistook for a prostrate body, but no sign of the missing horse.

'If you say he's a black 'un he won't show up in the dark at all,' said the farmer. 'He's probably just standing by one of the hedges laughing at us. Better get some sleep now and look again in the morning. You'll find him all right then.'

'Do you really mean we can stay for the rest of the night?' asked Rebecca.

'Well, I can hardly turn you out on the road just as you are, can I?'

'I knew he wouldn't really,' said Rosamund. 'Not people who have horses, like us.'

'Though how on earth you think you can sleep in a straw hut beats me.'

'I wouldn't mind,' said Jane.

'I'd simply love it!' cried Rosamund. 'Oh, daddy, can we, tonight?'

'No you can't. Your mother and Grace will let me have it as it is for bringing you out in the fields so late.'

'Well, we'll be up early in the morning to help you look for Ebony.'

'I'm sure he's hung up somewhere,' said Holly miserably.

'Oh, no, he'll be all right,' said Rebecca. 'It's just that it's impossible to see a black horse in a black night. All the others are much lighter colours.'

18

The home-coming

BACK in the shed they took off their dew-soaked shoes and socks, and burrowed their damp feet into the warm straw. Before long steady breathing and intermittent snores told Holly that the other three, worn out by the long day, were sleeping soundly. Holly lay awake, straining her ears in case she should recognize Ebony's neigh. It was now comparatively quiet outside. The horses had settled down and the owls had fled. Only the squeaking of an adventurous mouse and the slow dripping of water sounded near at hand.

A number of pictures floated across Holly's disturbed mind: Ebony caught up in and lacerated by barbed wire; standing holding up a limp leg; drowning in a pond; or lying in a gully with his neck broken. Gradually these became confused with ones of Kelly with the plaster on his leg, and of her father battling to get Alaska into the truck. Just as her father was saying, 'You shouldn't have brought back a horse with white socks, they're always impossible to load,' she was awakened by the piercing crescendo of a cock greeting the dawn.

She sat up abruptly with a stiff neck and an aching head. The forms of the other sleepers were just visible in the faint light seeping in through the cracks. Rebecca half sat up and fell back again; Clive turned over with a grunt; Roy did not move. Drawing on her damp shoes Holly crawled to the door and let herself out as silently as possible. The world lay grey and dew-drenched under a pale grey sky. Even the colour of the tiled roofs was dimmed by dew. The cock, perched on a post of the cow-byre, glared at her suspiciously with gold-rimmed eyes,

while his Light Sussex wives gathered hopefully round in case
she was in charge of their breakfast.

As she went down the track the mist in the valley struck cold
on her face and hands. The pony in the orchard whickered, and
she glimpsed his stocky chestnut figure peering through the
hedge at her. Baynard, Sarah, and Alaska were standing with
their backs to the hedge gazing meditatively across the valley.
Her hope that Ebony would be with them was blighted.

'You saw him last – you must know which way he went,' she
said.

They blew on her cold hands, and finding no titbits turned
away. Holly roamed the three fields, looking for gaps in the
hedges and finding none. In the bottom field the cart-horses,
mild and inoffensive by the morning light, were feeding undis-
turbed. The rising sun caught the oast-house cowls and the
higher trees in its rays, and more cocks began to crow cheerily
along the valley. While Holly was wondering dispiritedly where
to look next she heard a horse neigh a few fields away. The
three horses pricked their ears and looked in the direction from
which it had come, but if it had been Ebony she felt they would
have answered. All the same, she climbed over a place in the
hedge which had been made up with poles, and found herself
in a hop garden where the new strings formed a kind of brown
mist beneath the wirework. The first thing she noticed were
some hoof-prints in the loose damp soil. They were round and
rather large, and she at once recognized them as having been
made Ebony. With leaping heart she followed them at a
jog-trot.

It was not easy to distinguish them all the way, for Ebony had
wavered about, apparently pausing to nip a shoot from the
hedge or wandering out into the garden to sample a hop bine.
At the corner of the garden several of the strings were broken
as if he had blundered into them in the dark. Holly traced him
thus through two hop gardens and into a third, which curved
round the side of a small wood. Here a row of hopper huts
faced on to a strip of turf beside the wood. An open fire burnt
on the green, some bright but ragged washing flapped from a

line, and an old brown horse grazed near by, tethered by means
of a chain and a strap round his neck. Holly had come upon
the temporary headquarters of a family of gipsies, there for the
hop-training season. For a second her heart sank again, thinking
that it must have been the old horse whose tracks she had been
following. Then she saw Ebony, tied to the hedge between two
blocks of huts.

He's been stolen by the gipsies! The thought leaped instantly
to her mind, and at the sound of voices she slipped behind one
of the empty huts. Already a plan of rescue was forming in her
head. She would creep between the hedge and the backs of the
huts until she got to Ebony, release him, and send him off with
a smack, trusting him to find his way back to his companions,
while she herself tried to escape in another direction.

Without wasting another second she started to put the plan
into action. The huts were arranged in pairs with narrow gaps
between, and there were two such gaps to be crossed before
reaching the place where Ebony was tied. By the voices she
guessed that the gipsies were sitting in front of the hut just
beyond him. The first gap was crossed safely, but at her next
dash the old brown horse started and rattled his chain.

'What's that?' exclaimed a voice quite close. 'What scared
'im, Joe?'

Holly lost her head on finding the gipsies closer than she had
thought. She dashed for Ebony's head, startling him too, so
that he drew back and dragged his rope taut. She had hardly
begun to struggle with the knot when what seemed to be a pack
of dogs hurled themselves upon her with yelps and snarls. Some
one yelled at the dogs, but not before a brindled lurcher had
leaped against Holly and knocked her into the hedge. Ebony
plunged on the end of the rope, causing the branch to which it
was tied to lash violently. By the time Holly had picked herself out of the hedge the noise of the dogs had died away and
she found herself surrounded by an old crone, a young woman
with vivid yellow hair, a man, and several children.

'There, there, lidy,' said the yellow-haired woman. 'You're
not 'urt, are yer? They wouldn't 'arm a fly, them dogs, but you

set 'em off coming so sudden. Quiet, Lin! Joey, tie Bess up.'

One of the children dragged away the brindled lurcher, and the other dogs sat down and scratched themselves – there had been only three after all.

'But you've got my horse,' Holly blurted out.

'I guessed you've come for 'im,' said the man. 'We was going to bring 'im back up the farm when it got later.'

'Oh, but how did you know we were at the farm?'

'Oh, we knows,' said the man, grinning amiably. 'Making enough row you was last night. Your 'oss turned up 'ere early this morning. Come over that 'edge lovely, 'e must 'ave. You can see the marks down there where 'e landed.'

He undid Ebony's rope and handed it to Holly. Ebony instead of nuzzling her gratefully, tugged at her until he got his head over an untrampled piece of grass and began to feed.

'You sure you can manage 'im, lidy?' asked the woman.

'Oh, yes, thank you,' said Holly.

'Course she can. Do anything with an 'oss, that young lidy, I'll bet,' said the man.

It occurred to Holly that this flattery might be designed for a special purpose.

'I'd give you a present,' she said awkwardly. 'But honestly I haven't got a single thing on me.'

Perhaps her appearance gave credence to this statement, for the gipsies only laughed good-naturedly.

'That's all right, lidy. We works for the gentleman up there, and 'e's good to us while we're 'ere.'

By the time Holly and Ebony got back to the farm everybody was up and about, cows were being milked, the cart-horses had been brought into the stable, and Grace was throwing grain to a mixed flock of hens, ducks, and geese.

'There you are!' she exclaimed. 'They're out looking for you, and breakfast'll be on the way in five minutes. I told 'em I'd ring the bell if you got back before they did.'

She tossed out the last of the grain, and taking a big hand-bell off the window-sill swung it with a zest that sent the notes clanging across the valley.

'That'll fetch 'em! So you found the horse all right? Well, that's one thing to be thankful for. Put him in the stable, and then come and sit by the fire and dry your soaking feet.'

Holly delivered Ebony over to the charge of the carter, who announced his intention of giving him 'a bite to eat', and was sitting by the kitchen fire when the others returned.

'You might have warned us you were going off like that,' said Rebecca. 'We've been very worried over you.'

'I wasn't,' said Roy. 'I knew old Holly wouldn't come to any harm. Where did you find Ebony?'

'Some gipsies found him in the hop gardens, and tied him up by their camp.'

'The Sweeneys, of course; why didn't I think of them!' said the farmer. 'They know everything that goes on round here. But how did he get into the hops?'

'They said he jumped the hedge.'

'Must be a pretty good jumper then – it's not low anywhere along there. How does he go hunting?'

'I don't know. I've only had him about two days. But he jumped a dike yesterday.'

'But I thought the children said you'd been touring for some time?'

'We have, but you see, Ebony isn't the horse I started out on,' and Holly unfolded the story of the exchange.

'My word, you've taken something upon yourself!' exclaimed the farmer. 'What's your father going to say to it?'

'That's what she's waiting to find out,' said Roy.

'What would you say if Jane or Rosamund changed their pony for another without consulting you?' asked Rebecca.

'Make them change it back again double quick.'

'But if it were ever so much better than the original one?' pressed Holly.

'Well, I really don't know. It would be rather a poser. I dare say I'd let them keep it in the end. But I hope you won't put the idea into their heads.'

The farmer's final reply gave Holly a ray of hope over her own problem. She felt that if only she could persuade her father

to let her keep Ebony for at least a little while he would eventually come round to letting her have the black horse for good.

'Breakfast is ready!' called Jane at that minute.

'We've been invited to breakfast,' Rebecca explained to Holly.
'Jolly decent, isn't it, after all the trouble we've caused. It seems
they know Clive's people.'

'They buy our day-old chicks because they're the very best
for miles,' said Clive.

Clive assumed a new importance in the eyes of his companions, and this was further increased when they saw the breakfast to which they had been invited. It was almost like being at
home to sit in the low-beamed room eating bowls of porridge
and cream, eggs, bacon, and tomatoes, and as much toast and
home-made marmalade as they could find room for. By the light
of day the farmer, divested of his town-going clothes, and
wearing an old tweed coat and breeches, bore a much more
homely aspect.

'I dare say I sounded a bit cross last night,' he said, serving
them large helpings. 'The fact is, I'm a real country bumpkin,
and a day in London frays my temper. Now tell us some of
your adventures; Jane and Rosamund are all ready to lap them
up.'

While they were reciting some of their doings the farmer's
wife came down to breakfast, bringing an odour of throat pas-
tilles and inhalant.

'To think all this was going on and I didn't hear a word of it
last night!' she exclaimed. 'That comes of taking aspirins! And
then they let you sleep in the straw house – if only I'd been
about we could easily have found enough beds for you.'

'Oh, but it was much more fun for them,' said Jane. 'They're
like us, they just love doing *odd* things.'

'Do you expect to be home today?'

'Yes, we've only about twenty miles to do,' said Roy, who was
never long separated from his maps.

'Daddy,' said Rosamund eagerly, 'can we go with them some
of the way and show them the short cuts through the hop
gardens?'

'If you promise on your honour to turn back when you get within sight of Bodiam. No ideas of spending the night out, or anything like that.'

'Goody, goody! I'll go and get Mike.'

'Mike is the butcher's pony,' explained Jane. 'He lets us have him for two whole days each week.'

By the time the others had groomed and saddled up Rosamund had reappeared with a little roan cob which she assured them could trot faster than any other pony.

'But we're not allowed to let him go his fastest because it makes him bad to drive. Once he met the hounds and ran away with the cart, and everybody's joints got spilt out along the road.'

Jane and Rosamund took great pride in being able to conduct the others through the hop gardens along the Rother valley, here a very small river indeed.

'You wouldn't find your way by map,' they told Roy, ' 'cos some of them aren't real footpaths at all.'

Once they were startled by a very small train with a tall funnel, one carriage, and a couple of trucks chuffing with a disproportionately large amount of hissing and whistling through the lazy countryside.

'Simon's actually been by that train,' said Jane. 'Daddy bought him off some men at a fair who were knocking him about.'

'He must be glad to live with you now,' said Holly.

'Oh, yes, he is. But it's left a mark on his memory, you know. Sometimes he looks very serious indeed, and then we know he's thinking of the awful life he had before he came to us.'

At Bodiam they took their leave of the two little girls, who stood on the hump of the bridge and waved until they were out of sight.

'Are we in Kent now?' asked Clive as they clattered across the river, the horses' hoofs sounding hollow over the bridge.

'Not yet,' said Roy, glad to be in charge of the route again. 'Not until we've crossed the Kent Ditch.'

'That doesn't sound much of an obstacle,' said Holly.

Bodiam Castle rose before them on the fringe of the narrow

marsh. Their path lay round the edge of the moat, and their reflections moved among the water-lilies and the turrets of the castle whose great stone walls rose sheer from the water. Although the others lingered to count the many towers and watch the busy darting jackdaws that lived in them, Holly, for once, urged them on. She was all eagerness to get across the Kent Ditch. This she expected to be something rather straight and newly dug with drainpipes somewhere in evidence, but it turned out to be a shallow mill-stream meandering by a disused water-mill and through a bluebell coppice. The road bridge crossed it near a pool, where little boys were fishing from the bared roots of a tall pine.

'Out of Sussex into Kent!' chanted Clive as they rode over the bridge.

They were in their home county at last, and they urged the surprised horses up the next hill at a rousing trot. Another mile or so brought them within sight of Sandhurst clock tower facing with a cheerful grin across the village green.

'Why, I've been here before!' exclaimed Holly.

'I expect you have; we've only about ten miles to go now,' said Roy. 'What about dinner?'

'I couldn't eat a thing,' said Clive.

To their surprise they all found that for once their hunger was in abeyance, due either to the particularly large breakfast they had enjoyed at the farm, or to the excitement of finding themselves so near home.

'They're bound to give us a good feed when we get home, so perhaps we'd better save up for it,' remarked Roy.

'Are there any more bridle-paths?' asked Rebecca.

'There is one we ought to be able to follow along the marsh from Newenden.'

'That's good,' said Clive, ' 'cos Alaska's shoes are really on their last legs.'

'Sarah's are as thin as paper, but I think they'll just last home.'

At Newenden, a tiny village tucked in under the hillside, they came upon the Rother valley again. The green turf over which the bridle-path ran roused up the horses' spirits, and as if sensing that they were near their journey's end they cantered along without urging. Stopping only to open gates, they covered the widening arm of marshland rapidly. At Potman's Heath the bulky Isle of Oxney, an island only when the winter floods surrounded it, was all that lay between them and Romney Marsh. Holly fell unusually silent when she saw the hilly outline of the island rising before them. In little more than half an hour's time they would be turning into the yard at Haffeneys, and thinking of this moment gave her a disturbing mixture of excitement and dread.

There was always a thrill in coming home from a journey of any length, and in particular from this one, which had brought them step by step across half the width of England. Yet with every stride Ebony carried her the enormity of his very presence seemed to grow. When she first encountered him at Arundel, to exchange him with Crumpet seemed the obvious and sensible thing to do, but now, in her home surroundings, the action seemed quite preposterous. She stroked Ebony's neck, where it was hot under his mane, while his head bobbed before her in time to his busy step, and his ears pricked to and fro as he took an intelligent interest in what he passed. The thought of his being sent to a sale yard, and tied up with a string of others with numbers stuck on their backs to be knocked down without a reserve to any gipsy or dealer, brought the tears to her eyes. Surely her father could not be as hard-hearted as all that? For the hundredth time she rehearsed the list of Ebony's virtues: 'He doesn't kick, bite, buck, or rear, or shy at traffic—'

'Whatever are you mumbling to yourself about?' asked Roy.'

Sarah, suddenly aware that she was almost home, had quickened her paces and caught up with Ebony.

'I bet you're wondering what your father's going to say when he sees Ebony,' said Clive from the other side.

'Oh, don't bother me!' cried Holly, sounding crosser than she meant to.

'Well, you'll soon know the worst. That tree with the dead

bit on top grows on our land. Good old Sarah, you'll deserve a bit of a holiday after this!'

'I think I'll still ride Alaska a bit every day. Now that she's just got right it would be a pity to let her get back to being uppish again.'

'Baynard could do with at least a week off,' said Rebecca. 'The constant journeying with only what grazing they could pick up on the way seems to have told on him more than the others. It must be having a bigger frame to nourish. But he's got several weeks to recover in before he goes home.'

Holly envied the confidence with which the others spoke of the immediate future.

Now they were coming down the steep lane that twisted like a corkscrew, and first the tops of the wych-elms along the canal bank and then the low horizon of the Marsh itself came into view; last of all the tiled roofs of Haffeneys. The cows were crossing the bridge back on to the Marsh, and a bent figure in shirt-sleeves hobbled behind them.

'Hallo, Josh! We're back!'

'Can see that for meself.' Joshua straightened and supported himself on his stick while the cows streamed on their accustomed way. 'And rare peaceful it's been without you; the more's the pity it doan last.' Then his eyes fell upon Ebony. 'Sakes! So that's the hoss? What does a gal like you think you know about hoss-dealing?'

'What does daddy think about it?'

'It ain't for me to say what Mr Granger thinks. I only know what I'd do if I was him.'

Not wishing to hear something that would certainly be unpleasant Holly rode into the yard with the others close behind. They were all anxious to witness Ebony's reception. Cecil, tinkering with a disk-harrow, was the next to greet them.

'Hallo, glad you've got back OK, because it means I've won my bet with Bert.'

'You've been betting on us?'

'Well, you know what a gloomy bloke Bert is, and he said you'd be certain to have some trouble with the gees an' have to hire a truck home. But I told him you kids were tough and would get them gees home s'long as they had a leg between the lot of 'em. Find the hostels all right?'

A hoarse neigh from behind the barn drowned their reply, and was instantly answered by Sarah, who after all had not forgotten her old friend Kelly. Ebony made straight for the water tank outside the cowshed as if he had known his way about the farm all his life, and the riders jumped down and let the other horses follow suit.

Home once more. Holly looked round the farm, so strikingly familiar after all the new places they had visited, and decided in a flash that it was the best one they had been in yet. But where were her mother and father? If they were out there would be unbearable tension. However, the neighing of Kelly and Sarah had acted like a bugle call. The back door flew open before Mrs Granger, and Mr Granger appeared at a jog-trot from the dairy.

'So you're really back at last! Oh, I am glad to see you! No broken bones, or colds, or scars of any kind?'

That was Mrs Granger as she kissed them all round.

'I kept telling you they'd be all right,' said Mr Granger, plainly just as relieved as his wife to see them safe. 'In fact they all look better than when they started out, barring a bit of dirt. And here's the infamous black horse.'

This was the moment to unroll Ebony's list of virtues, but it found Holly speechless. She only nodded and stroked Ebony's nose, and it was actually Rebecca who said:

'He's rather a nice-looking animal, isn't he? And he's settled down quite a lot on the ride, much better than I thought he would.'

Her simple statement released a flood of qualifying ones. Holly promptly remembered all she had rehearsed so often during the last few miles, and Clive and Roy butted in with the same things in different words. Ebony, sensing himself to be the centre of interest, poked his nose from one person to the next under the impression that this must mean something to eat.

Mr Granger looked utterly incredulous.

'Such a paragon of a horse never was to be had for less than a couple of thousand pounds!'

But a great deal of his disbelief was put on, and to hide this fact he busied himself feeling the horse's legs and looking at his teeth. Then he told Holly to mount again and jog up and down the yard. This might have been unfortunate in view of Ebony's refusal to stand alone while being mounted, but Roy slyly put out a hand on the off side and held the bridle. Ebony liked an audience, and showed himself off well.

'He goes gaily enough,' said Mr Granger. 'What about on the turf?'

But here Mrs Granger intervened.

'If he's brought Holly all the way back from Arundel there can't be much wrong with his paces. For goodness' sake let's get these children indoors and washed and fed!'

'I suppose you're right,' said Mr Granger disappointedly. 'Do you know if he can jump?'

'Ooh, yes!' They all reassured him on that point.

'And what was this mention of bolting? Nothing more's been said about that.'

'Well, you see, he hasn't really done it seriously since we left Arundel.'

This conversation took place while they were unsaddling.

'I suppose I'd better be going on,' said Clive, sounding tired and rather flat.

'Of course not; you and Rebecca are to make a night of it here,' said Mrs Granger. 'We'll phone up your homes and tell them you're safe.'

'Yes, we ought to celebrate our last day's travel,' said Roy. 'Gosh, I'm simply starving!'

'Well, I've been cooking against your return for the last two days.'

'Daddy, you haven't actually said,' implored Holly.

'Said what?'

'About Ebony, of course. He won't have to go to a sale, will he?'

'I'm afraid there aren't any horse sales advertised just now. You could, of course, send him up to Tattersalls.'

'Oh, daddy!'

'Or to the Elephant and Castle sale yard.'

'It's not really fair to go on like that, uncle,' said Rebecca, seeing Holly's strained expression.

'Well, I thought perhaps that now Holly's got a taste for horse-dealing she might like to go on and change him for an even bigger and better horse.'

'Oh, daddy, I knew you were joking *really*, but I wasn't quite sure. Then I can keep Ebony?'

'Yes, if you feel quite happy about him. Your mother, for once, showed more horse-sense than I did when she said after Rebecca's ring-up that if the horse brought you along safely all the way over the downs from Arundel, as well as along the roads, it would be as good a test as any. But I don't mind telling you we've had some pretty anxious moments wondering how you were getting on.'

'If you don't come in soon tea will be spoilt,' announced Mrs Granger.

So they led the horses up to the field and turned them out with Kelly. The old cob showed his excitement by trotting round, a little hobbily on his bad leg, with his bobbed tail straight up in the air. Claiming Sarah in a lordly manner, he sent Baynard and Alaska off to the far side of the field, and Sarah, realizing that she was home, meekly accepted her old position. Then Kelly made some passes at Ebony, but he refused to be intimidated. Turning his back on Kelly he stood his ground and resolutely went on feeding, saying plainly enough by his attitude: 'It's no good you waggling your head, old chap, I've come to stop and you'll have to get used to me.'

Back in the house Mrs Granger was setting out the feast she had been preparing for days. And after several big kettles of hot water had removed the worst of the dirt they all sat down to, among other things, cold chicken and ham, and a trifle consisting mainly of cream and blanched almonds. Even with this before them they found time to talk, to ask questions, and to tell travellers' tales. The words bubbled and eddied with gusts of laughter, while the four stretched their legs under the table, and felt none the worse for the thought that there was no long ride before them on the morrow.

'I still can't think how you managed on the money,' said Mrs Granger. 'We were expecting an S O S several days ago.'

They looked triumphantly one to another.

'Oh, we told you it wouldn't cost an awful lot.'

'Though it was a pretty near thing at the end,' added Rebecca with feeling.

'But it was all a complete success,' said Clive. 'There's no doubt about that.'

'In fact you're all quite sorry to be home again.'

'Oh well . . .' This was something of a poser, for they were not sorry at all.

'It's funny,' said Roy, 'but there are a lot of things to do with home I hadn't thought much about before. Coming nearer, and finding our way day by day, has somehow made it seem an exciting sort of place.'

'It's always a good place to come back to,' said his father.

Holly remembered these comments when she went to see how the horses were settling down just before dusk. The old barn owl, who had lived at Haffeneys longer than any of them, was just setting out on his hunt over the Marsh, and the moor-hens down on the canal were calling in their chicks. In the Barn Field Baynard and Alaska still kept apart, while Sarah, Kelly, and Ebony were feeding close together, which was how they should be now that Haffeneys was home for Ebony too.

These are other Knight Books

THE HERON RIDE
Mary Treadgold

On a warm, summer evening, at sundown,
Sandra and her brother Adam stood in a cottage
garden, watching a line of riders cantering
across the skyline of the Downs. Sandra, for
whom life had been tough and sad, longed to be
riding with them. But for her there was no
horse, and there was no money.

This is the story of how she and Adam became
so involved in the fortunes of these six riders
that, in the end, her luck turned.

THE GOOD MASTER
Kate Seredy

The famous story for boys and girls of all ages
about life and hard riding on the Hungarian
Plains, newly illustrated by the notable artist
Imré Hofbauer.

Ask your local bookseller, or at your public
library, for details of other Knight Books, or
write to the Editor-in-Chief, Knight Books,
Arlen House, Salisbury Road, Leicester,
LE1 7QS.